David Dordi

INDIFFERENT

www.novum-publishing.co.uk

All rights of distribution, including film, radio, television, photomechanical reproduction, sound carrier, electronic media and reprint in extracts, are reserved.

Printed in the European Union, using environmentally-friendly, chlorine-free and acid-free paper.

© 2016 novum publishing

ISBN 978-3-99048-318-3
Editor: Nicola Ratcliff, BA
Cover photos:
Wektorygrafika, Ashestosky,
Alex Malikov | Dreamstime.com
Cover design, layout & typesetting:
novum publishing

www.novum-publishing.co.uk

Prologue

At the beginning of time, roughly after the earth was just created. God sitting on his throne only his white robes were possibly visible. He was making a man in heaven. Heaven sparkling white, slightly cold and warm but it was completely empty with God's hands colliding and dancing together. Until his hands separated together, opened up and spread out proud of his latest creation of a human being, his mouth opened "Warrior" He was placed in Earth. The man saw the magnificent waterfalls, the lush green grass and the organic structure of trees with their barks so radiant. Over in the distance, he saw something strange engulfing earth like a black cloak, lying above earth as it spreads, it looked strange like some kind of darkness. His heart heavier, over the fact that these beautiful creatures are being scared and running away from this dark cloak. He had desire to fight and God heard his favour God willingly gave him an army of people with the man. The man said to God "Thank you but I need something to fend off evil, away from my brothers and sisters for a long time." "I will give you the power of strength and immortality of a dragon. The eyes of a hawk and a mind of a wise man." When evil was creeping on Earth and engulfing it with darkness, he stood stiff as a solider, looking at the darkness eating whatever it sees in its path he stood tall and mighty to protect everyone like a ray of light in the darkness. Unsure to what the darkness was they went in it without remorse and knew defeat was no option. The battle was long and God's army had to fight as it was their destiny to protect their home Earth. Once it was over, the army triumphed greatly sweating blood dripping from their skin understanding pain. God told them they are free to live in peace and harmony without fear of evil over them. Shocked and scared as the leader didn't know where to go in his life but as time passed he found a beautiful woman and fell in love. They had two boys who were blessed with the names, Dante and Enzo. God was so pleased that the leader had moved on that he invited both of them to the kingdom of Heaven, but at a price. He had to leave their sons at the hands of God. God wanted them to go to a specific time and location, as he had plans for them. The army on the other hand were angry, because they had felt they were abandoned and evil had got a hold of them. The army started plans on ruining the creation of Earth and the people. They ran away and patiently started their plan.

Being strayed away from the order of God's army, they caused chaos. They were called Ancient humans at the place in heaven they were most feared in history. They were the lost souls. They were the Spartans, the most feared combatants of History. In the Russian history Rasputin was poisoned, drowned and even beaten to death but nothing happened until they burned him and had to watch him. They wondered where he got his mysterious healing power. Historians believed it was medicine to hypnotize the Tsar Nicholas ll's son but the truth was, that he was an ancient human with incredible healing power. Hitler, a human that was controlled by an ancient human until he made a mistake that the ancient human wasn't there to tell him what's right and wrong, thus the allies won the Second World War. But what was the plan? What was their goal in which they tried for so long?

God feared his creations were in danger and knew that it was time to act, as the ancient humans were prepared to set their plan in motion. God sent the leaders' sons to an orphanage, knocked on the door and left in a blink of an eye. He sent them to earth at the present time so that both of them would be taught to defend the earth from an ancient human era. They called the plan the Apocalypse.

Centuries later

A Moment's Grace

It was the break of dawn and it was getting dark with the moon shining brilliantly in the sky. Driving in their silver car, in which the seats were black and quite stiff. The atmosphere in the car smelt like dust in the air with the windows rolled down. Dante the elder brother whose skin tone differs to Enzo but they didn't even mention it, as they knew they were the same blood as he was brown. He is a little shorter than his younger brother, but he is physically built without abs. He has quite short hair and liked to shape his hair in a modern style. Enzo was lighter in skin tone. Thin built figure who liked to work on his body, in which he had the complete set of abs, arms and a good body shape. Both their eyes were brown, with Dante having black hair and curly but Enzo having slightly brown hair when he appears in the sun otherwise it would tend to be black His hair was straight not like Dante's. Enzo finished college and wanted to talk to their old man. They call him old man as they would love to annoy their foster father who took them in when he found them on their doorstep. He looked around forty to fifty years and wore glasses, had stubbles for a beard and his hair was long and slicked back. His hair started getting white, it looked like salt and pepper. He lived with four other priests. Dante and Enzo wanted to say their last goodbye to their father before they applied to university. But when they arrived at the orphanage, it was destroyed. The door was smashed open, the tinted windows of pictures were smashed with holes as well. Their old man Quinton, was lying on the floor with blood everywhere around him wearing his blood stained, cracked eyeglasses along with a strap. A humongous void near his heart, also the other priest bodies were splattered everywhere. Quinton heard footsteps in their broken down home, and in his dying breath he said "Enzo, Dante" with regret in his eyes, as he didn't want his sons to look at him like this. He tried to turn his pale looking head as the light from the moon touching his skin from different areas but most of the light touched half of his face. Enzo and Dante grabbed both of his hands. His icy cold fingers "I want you to go to south east and go to the edge of town. Go to the dark alley and there is a phone booth," with each word, he struggled with his dry lips, trying to lick them to keep them warm for him. "Open the letter and read it." He paused and looked at their heartbroken eyes, tightening their fists to provide him warmth and contentment. "I am sorry." Quinton's striking eyes pierced Dante's soul and he remembered that Quinton was there for his first day of school marching into class like a trooper. Enzo remembered when he cried in class because he felt so alone in his life and the teacher had given up on him and shouted "Let him cry". Quinton saw to it that every day he showed his face through the window, to make him feel good again and arrive always five minutes early to his school. Whenever he would leave with Quinton, Enzo would stick his tongue out at his teacher before leaving. Dante and Enzo looked at each other and realised that they only have each other to look after now. Enzo miserably said "We need to leave!" Dante looked at him with sadness in his eyes and said "Okay."

Getting up, Quinton's icy hand grabbed Dante's hand tightly and said "Be careful my sons, you are the only hope," he continued decaying "My only hope." Dante kneeling "Come with us Quinton. I will take you to the hospital."

"Don't be rash, it struck near my heart."

"Tell me who did this to you?"

"Don't be reckless and start beating up people Dante."

"Don't die!"

"I am in no condition." Said Quinton.

His hand slowing getting weaker and unable to grasp Dante's arm.

Enzo fell down on his knees and grabbing him shouted "Dad!"

Dante stood up clutching Enzo shoulder "Let's go, we both know it's dangerous to stay here now."

Enzo got up and walked out slowly with Dante. As Enzo got out of the door Dante looked at Quinton's corpse "I will not forgive whoever has done this to you Quinton and everyone here."

They didn't shed a tear as Quinton had trained them for this moment that they were never prepared. They walked out in silence, honouring his last moments and his funeral.

The Other Side

Sitting down on a chair, was an utterly mysterious man blocked from the outside world. The room was completely dark. Pitch black. The only source of light was the massive window behind him, with the red sun shining. His black chair facing towards the sun, admiring it. A man went in the office and sat down on the red leather designed sofa. The man sat down gently with confidence of the man behind the black chair.

"Did you complete the Job?"

"Yes sir."

"Did you kill the two boys and Quinton?"

"Yes Sir," he hesitated "but!"

"But? Are you saying you didn't complete the job?"

"Quinton is dead but the-"

"The boys are alive!" He yelled.

The man flinched, as he slightly moved the chair, but readjusted it looking straight.

"It's fine, mistakes happen."

"I are really sorry sir."

"But they are boys, what destruction they will cause?"

"They are no ordinary boys. But it's fine. I will give you a chance because you completed it fast."

He pulled out the knife, waving it around with his hand with the man clearly seeing it.

"What is the meaning of life?"

"Death?"

He threw the knife at the hitman. He slightly tilted his head cutting his cheek slightly.

"Hmm!" He said. "Well, you are right."

"Why throw a knife at me?"

"I wanted to see if you were ready for death."

"I was ready when I accepted the job to kill a paladin."

"Good man."

"Can I please leave?"

"Sure, the money has been wired to you." he said "Before you leave I need you again."

He reached into his pocket, but did it slowly as he was aware the man he was dealing with wasn't like any ordinary multi billionaire he had dealt with before. He knew he was different, like himself. He pulled out his card and tossed it at his desk.

"I do not want your card."

"How will you get in contact with me?"

"I have my sources."

"Yes?"

"Was it hard?"

"I do not want to talk about my jobs." He said immediately interrupting his full sentence.

He got up without saying a single word and left the room.

The Road to Nowhere

Dante was driving with Enzo to where their father told them to go. It was a quiet street where they were driving, with a mixture of darkness and mystery in the air with no sign of life. Enzo was quiet the whole journey and Dante was full of a fiery passion for revenge. They ended up at an abandoned carnival.

The place was deserted. The atmosphere was chilling, it was quite dark with a moon covered by the clouds as it was their only source of light after they got out of the car. The merry go round was white but stained with dirt, or the paint had peeled off as the white horse without an eye looked quite frightening. The Ferris was quite old and rusted. The grass grew above the average height and wasn't cut. The path seems to be dusted by leaves everywhere. Getting out of the car and slamming the door Enzo grasped Dante's shoulder and whispered "Be Careful, I feel we are being watched."

"I can feel as if we are being watched as well, I was going to warn you too."

Both of them had to be cautious. Enzo noticed that there were people watching from the brushes and behind bumper cars. They managed to reach the phone booth, as it was located in the middle of the cross paths, it looked very strange as it was directly in the middle. Dante turned and discreetly looked at all his options of escape, "We're surrounded!"

"Quinton told us to come here for a reason."

Enzo pulled out his letter started reading it out loud for Dante to hear as well.

> My sons, there are many things you would like
> to tell me. Either I am dead or going to be.

> In the phone booth type the numbers
> 17/21/14/20/9/15/14
> And trust Mr. Cloud he will tell you everything
> and he will tell you what you are. I tried to protect you guys.
> But you will soon know your destiny.

Enzo was smart enough to work out that the numbers gave a hidden meaning. It spelt Quinton. He smiled slightly and feeling self-assured, he whispered "smart old man," as he typed in the numbers on the phone booth. They waited for a second until the phone rang. Dante stepped forward and picked it up "Hello there Cloud."

"You are not Quinton, you dirty walkers what have you done to him?"

"He is dead!"

"You are surrounded you dirty walkers with a sniper at the Ferris wheel. Twenty armed soldiers. I will not shoot you until you tell me where you got this number."

"He is dead and I am his son along with my brother and there is no sniper and only 3 armed guards outside."

Cloud ended the call. Enzo stepped out of the phone booth and looked at Enzo "That could have gone better."

Suddenly, Enzo shouted "Do not move Dante."

Dante looked at his chest and saw a laser pointing at his heart, the three soldiers relieved themselves with army paint on their face to camouflage themselves from the enemies. Both of them put their hands on their heads while, the soldiers came closer and put a bag on their heads.

Enzo's blindfold had been taken off. He closed his eyes as a bright light from above pointed at his face. The person left the room, as Enzo was looking at the room. He noticed it was like an integration scene. Enzo focused at the top of the wall and stared at it, he yelled "I know you are recording this, I can see the camera. I want to speak to Cloud." The door opened and with the blinding white light hitting his face, the figure of an average height man in black appeared. As he structured his eyes, he saw a middle aged man. He wore a priest's robe, just like Quinton. Enzo said, "Change of heart? Or did you read the letter?"

"I read the letter and I released your brother. I am sorry about the precaution."

"In the letter it talked about Dante's and my destiny. What is it?"

"I will answer those questions in time."

Dante was soon reunited with Enzo outside his interrogation room.

Cloud took them both to the theatre room. It was a massive stage with tons of people gathering, as audience in black uniforms as if they were wearing SWAT uniforms but without the helmets. They had guns that had been sheathed on their backs and side guns on their waists.

Stood on the centre of the stage with the brothers was Cloud he yelled "Brothers and Sisters, the end is near. These two young men are ancient humans."

They pointed their guns either at their heads. Enzo and Dante were confused to what the ancient humans were, they slowly raised their hands up.

Cloud shouted in anger "Do not shoot these young men. It's an order."

The party laid down their arms as cloud said "they are the protectors of this world."

The party got angry and yelled "They are killers. We should kill them before they kill us."

Cloud yelled "They are the ancient human leader's sons who protected this world."

"They are dangerous!"

"Quinton is dead! They are the only ones who can stop this war once and for all."

"Who is going to teach them?"

"I am!"

There were mumbles between the rebels.

"You are dismissed."

The rebels were dismissed but didn't give a sign that they could trust them.

Dante shouted "Who are we and what is this war?"

Cloud replied "Both of your destinies is to save this world, the ancient human era."

Enzo said "We are the sons of the ancient human leader?"

"Yes an ancient human is stronger, smarter, higher thinking capacity, faster and has the abilities to make them super humans but I will train you for that day."

Dante said "What Day?"

"Judgement day."

Sweat and Blood

Cloud gave them a room. Both of them went to their room and they were shocked to see it looked like a hotel suite, it was a spacious square room with everything that a hotel needed. The lights looked royal and there were two queen sized beds and a drawer between the two beds. Enzo said "I cannot believe this." Dante dropped his bags and said "We are doing this for Quinton's sake. He wasn't involved in all of this and got dragged into it and killed." With their room looking like a hotel suite with two beds, a sofa, television, fridge stuffed with food and drinks overnight. They were tired and decided to sleep.

Morning arrived and Enzo turned around and didn't find his brother in the other bed. He got up and decided to beat up any dirty soldiers who kidnapped his older brother. He wore his white inner shirt, a black shirt outside and trousers, as he opened the door, a woman stood outside as she was about to knock on the door. She looked down and slightly blushed, as she saw his face. She had blue eyes, black hair, and pale skin. Enzo noticed all of this and found that she looked beautiful. He didn't get distracted and said "Hi, have you seen my brother?"

"Yes, actually I am supposed to accompany you to the training area."

Enzo followed her and as they were walking, Enzo said "What's your name?"

"My name is Lilith."

"That's a beautiful name" he was trying to flatter her as he was very bad at flirting.

"Could you tell me what is this place?"

She said "We are at an abandoned organization base that has been rebooted by Benjamin a multi-millionaire company that is located away from the carnival you were taken from. That booth is a meeting point."

"What organization?"

"The organization that gave their life to save the world from the ancient human era but most of them had died due to this."

Enzo went quiet as they walked to their location. To give respect to those who lost their lives.

They arrived at a big door and as Lilith opened it, Enzo was shocked to see that the training room looked like a gym with dumbbells, weights, treadmills, pull-up bars, bench press, etc. Enzo heard yelps of cries and hostility. He noticed it was somewhat familiar and realised it was Dante. He shouted "where is that noise?"

"The door past the equipment."

Enzo rushed up to the door and with his fingers grasping the doorknob and his fingers tighten the warm doorknob, he opened the door and came to worry when he saw his brother bleeding on his head, where a cut had been opened near his temple, as he had been repeatedly punched and sweating. On one knee, inhaling to catch his breath and his one arm on the surface of the sand. It was a massive circle with sand filled and lights around. Enzo cried "Learn to fight back pussy."

Dante grasping his breath said "It's a bit tougher knowing we are going to fight the people who are going to destroy this world and Cloud it's not getting any easier."

Cloud said "Without weapons, it is easier to kill them by slicing their heads, shooting their heads or attacking the heart. You need to learn to break their arms."

"Time out!"

"Very well!"

Enzo and Lilith approached Dante a bit more closely.

Cloud said "You are in a team with other ancient humans with Lilith and two more you will meet."

"Were in a team of ancient humans?"

"Of Course! Since Enzo is here let's begin training again."
Enzo said "Isn't Lilith training with us?"
"No, she is done but she can surely watch."
Dante looked at Enzo and noticed that he had a little crush on her. He had a slight smug smile on his face and that he wanted to look good on her.

Lilith saw at the benches while Dante and Enzo were warming up. Cloud said "Ancient humans are immortal, they can heal easily but if you give multiple wounds, the healing factor has to spread and focuses at more than one point they cannot heal that much. They are immortal."

Cloud cut Dante's arm, it regenerated quickly. Enzo was fascinated about it.

Enzo said "Me and Dante do not have fighting experience against something that cannot die."

"There is a difference between immortality and invincibility."

"This is worse than a lecture."

"To kill your enemy, you must know your enemy. The head is the most effective way to kill them."

"Why the head?"

He pulled out a tablet from the training grounds' wall. It shows Greek signs of a man who is victorious in battle and who can heal but when he was challenged and struck a blow in the head, he died, thus leaving the human being called a hero, his name was Hercules, the first human to stand against the ancient human.

Cloud said "It was a long fight but he didn't give up. He used his hands that's why hand to hand is very effective."

"How could we kill them when we don't know how to control our superhuman strengths?"

"You are strong enough. I believe in you!"

Dante said "By our heightened senses?"

"Yes! Enough chit chat, let us fight."

Cloud stepped back and got into stance by stretching his leg forward and his arms shaping it into a palm as if, it was like he was a monk. Dante got into the same position and flipped him off.

Lilith started laughing. Both of them went in at the same time, but it quickly ended as Cloud got Dante's hand and dislocated it. Dante fell on the ground and screamed in pain. Cloud diverted his attention to Enzo, as he tried to kick Cloud he caught his leg and elbowed his knee and then his jaw. Pushed to the ground and snapped his leg. Enzo cried "Aaarrgghh!" Lilith got up.

Dante screamed "God, this hurts."

"I only dislocated them, I didn't break them."

Cloud approached Dante and got his hand and put it back together.

Lilith went to Dante and said "I got you sweetie."

"Did it hurt?"

"Of course it did hurt for me sweetheart."

"When you fell from heaven."

Lilith Blushed "Cliché".

Dante got up and said "I am going for a shower Enzo. Take care."

Dante left the room leaving Lilith and Enzo together. Enzo got up and said "After training, do you want to hang out?"

Lilith giggled and said "Aren't you bold asking a woman out."

"I want to know you, you seem interesting."

"I would love to."

"Where would I meet you?"

"Don't worry sweetie, I will find you."

Enzo and Lilith went their own separate ways. Enzo reached home and he saw his brother. Dante smiled and Enzo said "You heard."

Dante nodded happily.

Enzo said "I'm going to get some shut eye." as he jumped on his bed.

He smiled slightly and he shut his eyes.

Fierce Face, Sorrowful Soul

The Next Morning Cloud made them do physical training to increase the strength. They were fit but not enough for an ancient human. After time past, they learned how to fight against Cloud. Dante and Enzo went to the bar in which the revolutionaries were. Enzo and Dante sat down near the bar counter. There was little people there around three or four people. The bar was colourful and it was filled with drinks. With tall circular tables which you could stand and drink by and some had chairs. Dante said "I look so much buffer."

Enzo's face was filled with disappointment.

"What's the matter?"

"It's nothing."

"Girl problems."

"No!"

"So what is it?"

"Alright, it's Lilith I haven't seen her for a long time and it kind of bugs me."

"Ahahahaha, are you feeling alone?" he said, mocking Enzo.

"What's on your mind?"

"Actually, I'm just waiting for revenge to whoever killed our old me."

"Same here."

Dante got up and cried "Is it so hard to get drinks?"

Dante went away to find a bartender.

Suddenly Lilith shouted "Enzo!"

Enzo turned sharply and saw Lilith. She approached him "Is this seat taken?"

Enzo lied and said "No".

Lilith look at him with her elbow placed on the counter and her hands placed on her chin.

"So, you wanted to know me?"

"Of course."

"So where did you come from?"

"A priest took us in and raised us. He must be the same age as Cloud."

"You and Dante?"

"Yeah he said that he doesn't know who our parents were except we were from God."

"What happened?"

"The whole church got destroyed and we were going to go off to university and say our farewell."

Lilith was shocked "Go on?"

"Well, Quinton told us to come here."

"Wait! Quinton!"

"Yes, that's his name."

Her eyes showed fear gripping her soul "Do you know who Quinton was?"

"No, strange man, he mostly hung out with us and accepted smokes."

"He was a paladin."

"What is that?"

"A paladin is a person who is the highest rank of this army that stood against countless wars and survivors."

"I guess he never told us because he wanted to protect us. Was he the best?"

"He was the best, he was the strongest in what he did. After you and your brother came to his door, they knew that he was chosen by God to raise them."

"Well, yeah Cloud did mention that but we mostly ignored it, but he was right in the end."

Lilith saw Dante across the bar and saw him with the female bartender.

"Look at the bartender, she looks pretty cute, why not talk to her?"

Without hesitation "No chance."

"What, why?"

"I had a bad past Lilith."

"What happened?"

"I had a girlfriend and we were in love with each other. We wanted to go to the same university and get married." Said Enzo.

"And?"

"I had a stupid fight and I told her to die. I stormed out of our recently purchased dorm. I regretted my poor actions. I went to the flower shop and bought her favourite roses and went to the one cake shop that sold her favourite strawberry cheesecake."

Lilith biting her lip, her heart pounding with every nerve wrecking word, he said, "I rushed towards the apartment, but as soon as I arrived, the police were outside our dorm with a no enter sign. I didn't get a chance to check in but the police said there was blood everywhere and no body."

"Did they find the body?"

"No, they dropped the case and the body was still missing."

"How did you feel?"

"I cried almost every day and had a picture of her. When I used to sleep, I cried myself to sleep every time. I could handle the fact that we fought over such a stupid reason and that memory would play every time in my mind, where I wasn't able to be there to save her. After months, I was fine and we moved away from that area."

"Under that fierce face, there is a sorrowful soul." Lilith whispered.

"And Dante?"

"Well, Dante was a type, in which all the girls fell for him and they used to come to me to help themselves get closer to him, but he wanted to get into a law firm and start giving money to Quinton so he and the other priests would live well."

"Wow he has a pure heart."

"Well, he wanted to be a lawyer so he could help people but that surely went the wrong way because of this."

Dante came back and said "So you love birds doing fine?"

Lilith said "Yeah, See you tomorrow Enzo."

"Bye Lilith."

She kissed him on the cheek and said "I miss you too."

Enzo felt embarrassed because he realised that she'd heard his conversation with Dante.

Rebels will be rebels

In the training area, the brothers were training how to fight, with Enzo wrapping white fresh tape on his wrist, stretching the tape all the way to his hand and fingers. While Dante, with quick movements and his feet shadow boxing going back and forth with each jab and ending it with a swift hook to the face. Lilith was sitting on the benches, pointing her weapon at Enzo as she was trying to disguise her form, secretly looking at him as he tried to tape his fingers from time to time, he would try to catch a glimpse of her. They always try to stick together rather than mix with a crowd that they were well aware would usually end up in a fight or slaughter. Lilith avoided the rebels for a long time and she suggested that we also do not mix up with them. Most of them are mercenaries ready to die. Others have a personal revenge for the ancient humans' killing for families, in which they have abandoned all hope and will try to kill as much as they can. The rest of the rebels are doing it for money to either give back to their families for them to survive or some keep the money as the Benjamin co-operation pays a lot for a man to fight in war. Training with Dante as the boxing pads, Enzo's upper body strength was not a match for Dante or couldn't even be challenged to begin with. Punching in great succession with Dante lightly touching his head for any mistakes. Suddenly a group of rebels came in the training arena. "Sorry boys but it's booked for tonight." Dante spoke in a nice manner.

"Oh we know." The rebels smirked.

They got a metal bar and placed it between the handles of the door in case anyone tried to run away.

"What are you trying to do?"

"Nothing really," he said sarcastically "but I do want your death."

Lilith carefully looked, as she reloaded her weapon and took cover, listening to the conversation.

"Look we didn't touch you or offend you?"

"Yes but your presence irritates me."

"Fine." Enzo said.

"How about bare knuckle fight?"

"What?" Dante replied.

"You heard me!" Enzo implied "nine rounds of bare knuckle fighting."

"Sounds good to me." The rebel said.

The both of them went to the corner, Enzo whispered "He doesn't know."

"Know what?"

"He doesn't know that ancient humans are stronger."

"Or maybe he has a trick up his sleeve?"

"Dante slowly tilting his head as he looked at Enzo glaring. Avoiding eye contact as he left his brother."

They got to each corner with a silent signal, they knew they were ready and engaged in sparring. Dante fast and witted, managed to dodge all his dirty tricks, managing to give three shots on his face with a jab as a result, ending it with a deadly blow by ducking down his jab, slightly turning and rising up to a standing position, charging up his left hook, giving a devastating blow. Falling to the ground, as he spun in mid-air, his arms and legs flailing, as if he was a tornado. Touching the floor, as his head hit after the impact of falling down, with the sand spreading out as he slowly went down. Blood pouring out from his hair and busted wounds opened above his nose, as he coughed up blood, with each cough, the blood became thicker.

Dante got down on his knees, extending his arm, reaching it to the rebel fallen on the floor, as he tried to lift him up showing that he had a good fight to show sportsmanship. The rebel pulled out a knife from behind and stabbed Dante in the gut. Out of desperation, he kicked him back, pulling the knife out with all his might but it was stuck deep. He grabbed it with two arms, successfully yanking it out of him. Collapsing on his knees, as it was the first time he got stabbed. The wound healed rapidly as the rebel watched in amazement.

"Boys get the brother."

The other rebels held down Enzo, as things got worse, a rebel pulled out a dagger and placed it at his throat.

"What are you trying to achieve?" Enzo struggled.

"Look Dante," the mercenary said "Imagine your brother getting his throat slit again and again."

Dante was in a tight spot, as he knew that they would regenerate fast, but the pain will be too much to handle. The mercenary slowly stood up, trying to show that he was superior to Dante.

"Now round two?" he said happily, "But remember you don't want him to feel death?"

Dante knew he had to play defensive until he could either get help or to wear him down. Lilith knew shooting one of them would definitely be a problem. She steadily came out, sneaking her way through the benches and getting away but picking the metal bar out of the door. She ran to Cloud as fast as she could. Reaching to the door, she choked "Enzo and Dante are in danger."

"What kind of danger?"

"Level three."

Cloud pressed a button from under and got his katana and side pistol.

Dante deflecting punches and dodging his opponent, got frustrated and grabbed the dagger from the ground. Staring at each other as he tossed the blade from side to side, trying to perform little tricks to scare him off. He looked down on Dante, just because he must have killed one or two ancient humans. He started swinging the blade left and right, Dante dodging, keeping his momentum up. Until he got stabbed, pulling out the blade with blood flowing out of the wound, blood dripping from the blade with the blade shining on Dante's angered face. Kicked him to the ground and started stabbing him repeatedly. Enzo looked on in fear as he saw his brother taking the shots for him. It was like seeing a soldier covering the body of a child. Suddenly, the door kicked open as they were caught in the act. Cloud didn't need to question what was going on. He looked on with utter fury. Drawing out his weapon, shooting the two henchmen guarding Enzo. He forcefully gave his weapon to Lilith, walking slowly with his fist grabbing tightly, his sword extracted out his blade with his hair in a mess, as the blade sloppily hit each step as he went down.

"Cloud I can explain!" he said in fear. "He forced me."

"This is going to go one way," as he looked at him with his one eye covered by his sparkly white hair.

"Either I cut you up!" he implied "Or Dante gets to beat you to death."

"Please let me repent." he fell on his knees. "Please don't kill me!"

"Why would you touch my responsibility to protect these boys?"

"They are not welcome here."

"I am giving you one last chance."

Lilith ran towards Enzo, hugging tightly as she quivered on his shoulder. Dante looking at Cloud, knowing that in his eyes, the rebel was going to be a dead man.

"I got angry at the ones that have no family."

"I background checked you before I came here."

"Look in my …" he quivered in fear.

"Enough chances!" he shouted "I took the money sent to you."

"But …" he said.

He raised his arms above his head striking downwards, cutting his hand as it dived in the air reaching the cold sand with his ring and index finger, twitching as the sand dirtied the hand with sand marks on the bone of the hand as well on the full palm and fingers. Screaming in pain, quivered in fear as his legs were flailing on the ground, trying to push himself back as he saw his arm on the gold grainy sand, pushing himself away from Cloud. Eyes dilated, blood flying in the air, he placed his arm on his shirt, trying to stop the blood. Cloud swung his sword up, using all his might, as he suddenly stopped his blade with blood coming out of it. He saw some stains unable to be moved, so he wiped his blade with the index finger and the middle finger swiping his blade with the droplets of blood hitting the floor from his fingers. Velvet red stained his fingers as his eyes wanted to kill him badly but he wanted him to suffer.

"What if that blade hit his heart?"

"Cloud, please let me survive."

"We are past the point of forgiveness!"

"I want your blood to be spilt and you will be the example to those who touch them." As he pointed his fingers at Dante, Enzo and Lilith.

He slowly walked towards his with each step as the sand gripped his shoes from the trial of blood from his hand. He reached out the blade at the side of him, trying to protect himself, pointing it at Cloud's body shaken by fear, as he screamed with his second hand chopped off.

Screaming in pain, he showed his true self. Clouds eyes deceived him, as he couldn't believe what he saw. He saw the rebel's eyes go black for a split second and coming back to normal.

"You bastard." Quinton whispered "You think you could have fooled me."

The creature, shocked that Cloud predicted that he could have been one of them.

"What are you doing here?"

"We are here for the boys."

He placed his blade near his heart. Poking it slightly.

"Talk Lower creature." Cloud demanded "Or I will torture you."

"Cloud what is happening."

"Whatever you do." Cloud turned his head looking at them. "Do not come near me."

"Cloud"Lilith softly spoke.

"That is an order."

The creature breathing heavily said "That's all I know." He pressed his blade slightly more.

He removed the blade from his heart nearly poking it. He was relieved as he started breathing normally. Raising his leg and stomping his knee, screaming in pain and terror.

"You do not know anything." Cloud whispered.

He stabbed the blade in the heart of the creature, pulling his blade out and pushing it back in until he had reached conclusion that it was fully dead. Wiping the blade with his two fingers, he looked at Lilith as she covered her face on Enzo's shirt, with Dante looking at him with a face of mass confusion. Enzo looked at him, as if he was a sigh of danger for both Dante and Lilith.

"I can explain!"

"You slaughtered him."

"It is the enemy on our lines."

"So you mean it, an ancient human?"

"Yes but something was off about them."

"What do you mean?"

"I mean there was something not right." Cloud wondered "Maybe, just maybe."

"What is it?"

"I can't say but it was really difficult." Cloud said. "Any which way, let's call everyone here."

In a couple of minutes, standing in the middle, there they were, Cloud made a speech saying that all those who oppose him and the Benjamin company will receive death. They were being paid too much to fight in the battles and yet Cloud questioned their loyalty to him or the next generation of the freedom fighters who are destined to save the earth. But what was really on Cloud's mind is what had been bugging him. Have they evolved over the last years that he'd have fought with them? He thought maybe they were not ready to face an opponent who was siding with the side of the darkness. The rebels needed to be tested. He showed the body to the previous rebel who had betrayed him. He told them each and every detail to the point of cutting both his hands, breaking his leg and killing him but he didn't want to alarm the rebels or the next generation of fighters that they would possibly be in danger.

Paladin Training

Cloud was protecting everyone under his wing and he knew he had to prepare them in his study desk. He devised a training he was given to him and his four paladins in which they worked on survival, endurance, strength, stamina and lastly trust for each other. It was vital to understand these perks. He knew that if they were going to survive fighting a newly evolved ancient human they were as good as dead. Light shining on blueprints as his face as close to the paper writing down notes and sketching about the area of terrain they were going to go first. Finally when he got up he was finished and knew that this was one of the hardest paladin training that the other paladins along with him had difficulty with.

He wanted to surprise them but he had to be smart. He wanted them to have the real life experience in a real life scenario. Then it hit him. He got the key to both Lilith's and the brother's key. He went into the room and injected both of them and put sacks over their heads, tied them up with rope sitting on a chair. Cloud was quick, very quick. He didn't want any risks in the paladin's training, he knew that the drugs would wear off as any human who would have taken a sleep drug like that would had lasted them for three days but for an ancient human it would take three hours. Driving around in the van with Enzo being a light sleeper, the drugs wore off faster.

He got up with a blurred vision, with small see through holes, in which it looked like a galaxy through his eyes. Faded away, trying to stay away he felt something was wrong. Excruciating pain on his hip. Flexing his waist, pushing his hip up, shouting in pain "What the …" He was interrupted by Cloud pulling the sacks from off their heads, as he was at the back of the van catching the roof with both his hands at the back of the van standing "Morning sunshines!"

"Cloud what the hell you are doing!" Enzo shouted as he was always cranky when he wakes up.

"Well this is your training!"

"Training?" Lilith questioned.

"Paladin training."

"Oh no!" Lilith choked.

"What is this? Cloud unchain me right now," Enzo shouted.

"We are at a forest?" Dante said.

"Wow Dante you are rather calm."

"Answer my question!"

"Yes you are at a forest."

"So we have to survive?"

"No not just survive, but to get back here."

"So we don't know where we are?" Enzo said. "And you want us to get back home. Screw you!"

Cloud closed the van "Well this is the type of training I had. Take care and good luck."

Enzo looked at Lilith with her mind thinking with a serious face. Enzo didn't think talking to her was a choice. With his hands tied behind his back, he got up along with Dante.

"Dante Listen to me." Enzo said "I've got a plan."

"What is it?"

He got up and went behind Dante "Lilith check out our knots."

"Okay."

"They're different knots." Lilith said, sounding shocked.

"I knew it." Enzo.

Enzo underestimated Cloud, he didn't think he would think that far into detail. He knew that he wanted him to give up his arrogance from his sleep to benefit the team.

"Lilith I need you to tell me how to untie this knot." Enzo said.

"Okay."

She gave him directions on how to release the knot. In a matter of minutes, he managed to untie Dante's knot. Helping each other out was quick, they didn't want to waste time to make it dark. They didn't want to know the dangers that lure in the dark. Enzo didn't want anything to happen to Lilith, he was mostly more concerned with Lilith, as he knew Dante was smart enough. Dante looked at Enzo in silence and they understood each other as Dante started climbing the tree with his muscles flexing with each branch he caught. Getting on top of the tree, he saw clues in which he saw a passage. On his way coming down, he landed on tree trunks on his feet, then fell down, catching the same branch, swinging and landing on the one opposite it. Reaching the floor, he saw Enzo grabbing sticks with shark stones.

"Did you guys predict this?" Lilith questioned. "It has been ten minutes!"

"Quinton made us go camping."

"Camping?"

"More like survival or no food for today." Enzo said.

They formed spears and daggers, giving it to one another. They followed Dante with the course of direction.

Cloud waiting outside, the forest fences in property of Benjamin, looking at his watch, nodding in disappointment, "I thought you could have trained them Quinton." Cloud whispered.

"Of course he did." Dante smartly said.

"Wait what?" Cloud choked.

"Yeah, Quinton taught us a lot." Enzo implied.

"And we had a timer." Dante continued "Until we beat his record."

Cloud looked at his watch and was shocked. He froze at how they were able to react to situations and how well they cooperated with each other. He'd beaten Quinton's record of forty minutes.

He shouted "How!" They dropped the shivs as they went towards the van. "You coming Cloud?"

"But how!"

They explained that they got a slight sight of the fences and with the shivs, they cut whatever obstacles they continue to climb, with the advantages of the trees in which they were able to tell where they were going and how far. They made droppings, in case they got lost, just as a precaution, in case anything happened. If anyone got hungry, they chopped off bananas and sure that on one was hungry. They made sure they got good sources of water by lightly tapping it. To check if the water is bad or not they would usually drink from streams. Cloud was shocked at the fact that he treated the boys like his own sons rather than ancient humans, because he knew that if they drank dirty water, it wouldn't affect them but he made sure that if they had survivors, that they drink clean water. Cloud was proud. Proud of his bigger brother.

They went back home, eating good food, a lot of good food.

"This is delicious."

"Yeah," Lilith said, "you never gave us something so expensive."

"Wait!" He said with is mouth stuffed with salmon.

"Oh no!" Dante said.

"Don't tell me," Lilith choked "it's a trap!"

Dante fell first on his plate of food.

"Oh Shit." Enzo felt the drugs kick in and fell flat on his food.

Lilith threw the plate down before she fell down.

Cloud called in the rebels to pick them up and send them to another climate but this time it was a bit different.

They woke up in a completely different climate. They woke up in the desert. Sand surrounding everything, it was just hills, mountains and terrain of sand.

"That piece of shit!" Enzo whispered.

"What now boys?" Lilith said.

"I have no idea!"

"How about we go up that point of that sand mountain."

They manage to climb their way there. They saw nothing but barriers of sand.

"We need a stick."

Without asking any questions they followed Enzo's idea as the managed to get a stick from a malnourished tree breaking a twig Enzo took it and slammed it down to the ground casting a shadow from the ground. The looked straight and saw nothing but a barrier of sand.

"It is hopeless it is just sand." Dante said.

"Or does he want us to see how sharp our minds are." Enzo replied.

"I am with Enzo." As she went closer towards him.

"Alright let us go there."

In the blistering sun, they needed to cool down. They ripped off their shirts and mid-way for Lilith, as she was too embarrassed to go all the way. But Enzo tore his full shirt and gave half to her, to cover their heads from the sun. They would wrap the cloth around their heads, except their eyes. Enzo got thirsty, they managed to find some red berries and started eating them, using their ancient human inheritance to make them immune to all side effects. They reached a fence with Cloud with cold water in his hands. As they reached towards the fence and took the water from Cloud, without saying a word. Lilith came forward and slapped Cloud, "Don't you ever make me go through that again without giving me a day off." The brothers sided with her and knew that the training was intense enough. Trying to catch their breaths, with sweat pouring off them as Dante tried to wipe his face of the sweat. After drinking cold water, he then poured it down, flowing through his face feeling relaxed. They all knew they were not going to fall for the same tricks twice.

They went back home for the second time, but this time they were actually given a day of rest. They went to sleep for the first time without a training session. Enzo saw his long clean straight bed with the cushions fluffed up, the sheets nicely pressed and warm. Enzo looked at it as his only sign to relieve stress. As he laid his head on the pillow, he immediately went to sleep. He felt slightly cold covering himself, trying to wrap himself up, yet nothing seemed to have worked. He wanted to make sure that the heater was on. He felt uneven, as if he was sleeping on a hard surface. He slightly opened his eyes and saw he was in a cave that showed little light towards the matter, but there was a lamp inside the cave hooked and hung above them. "You piece of shit" he grunted softly, as he knew that Cloud had picked them up and lifted them all the way towards another god forsaken area in which they must either survive or die. Enzo likes to plan his course of action ahead of Dante, as he would like to read comics along with Dante, to think and always wanted to become someone like that, help other people. But, what they did was complete utter destruction towards that. He didn't really bother, as Lilith was next to him, trying to gather as much warmth as she could cuddling up next to him. He held her back, as her head started digging towards his chest and his head was place above her head as he gave her more of the bed sheets. He didn't want her to suffer, Enzo was a compassionate guy, he puts the needs of women above his own. Never knowing his father or mother, he taught himself that he must respect women even if he didn't know them and help people in their time of need. When he look at Lilith, the only thing he thinks about, is how he is going to protect her and how he is going to protect her from the harsh weather. He knew that there was some kind of meaning behind these stories. In the frozen wasteland with little protecting him, he made sure that he protected those who were valuable towards him. In the Rainforest, he knew that communication was key and vital to gathering his team together and all of them must pull their weight. If anyone doesn't pull their weight, either they die or be left behind. In the desert, with limited resources you must make the best use of it. Cloud tried to make sure that all of them had to use their time wisely, to ensure their safety, but both Enzo and Dante weren't much thinkers. They would usually go with their gut feeling, or hack or slash, or go through ideas of other people, to see how much they can gather. Enzo noticed all of this when he looked at Lilith.

Dante got up "What a surprise."

"I know."

"We need to get warmer." Lilith said. "At least we can control the warmth in our bodies."

"True." Enzo replied. "We could use the bed sheets."

"Oh my God!" Dante said "We've got only two!"

"Enzo and I will share one." Lilith said, "Take one for yourself."

Dante took a peek outside and noticed how terrible the weather was outside, it was freezing. They knew going out was going to kill all of them. Dante didn't want to try and test their superhuman abilities as what would happen if an incident broke out or an avalanche fell on them.

"Hey over here!"

They knew that they wouldn't be able to survive for long, as they knew that climbing up the trees would be impossible with all this snow coming down. It was affecting his morale. He thought maybe he couldn't do this, he looked down on the ground thinking what am I doing? Am I going down the right path? I should have continued to study and become a lawyer.

All these emotions mixed up within him. He didn't know anything about waging war on his enemies or about how to fight them. Then, he remembered he saw Quinton dying before his eyes. That is what made him thrive.

They were casually dressed and didn't have protection. Cloud knew that giving them protection with their superhuman abilities would be cheating. He knew that to get through this, he had to take a leap of faith. It was to do or to die in the snow.

"You ready?"

"Dante, maybe it is a bit risky!"

"Don't worry, that's the part of this mission."

"What do you mean?"

"Look ahead!"

They peeked their heads through and saw a slightly grey fence.

"We have to run through it." Lilith said.

"Yeah," Enzo replied, "we will heat up our bodies."

"Thus making ourselves a little warmer."

Taking a deep breath, as the over flowing steam came out of their mouths as they exhaled. Rubbing their legs and hands, with Dante covering the bed sheet over his head, Lilith and Enzo stared on and started running across the field of snow. Running and running, with pins and needles, attacking them under the sole of their shoes, as they tried to avoid hitting the trees, so the snow didn't fall on their heads or go down their necks. Even if they did hit the tree, the blanket would protect them. It was a stupid plan, but it was the only way. The exit was close, but it seemed so far. Lilith started to slow down. "Lilith what's the matter?" Enzo said, panting.

"I can't, it hurts."

Enzo told Dante to go ahead. He carried her on his back "hold on and take the full blanket."

Enzo running as hard as he could with the weight on his shoulders. Dante reached towards the finishing line. But he saw his brother in the distance. He ran back, ignoring Enzo's words.

"What are you doing here?" Enzo said.

"I came back for my little brother."

He picked her legs as Enzo got her arms. "Run backwards, we are really close." They started running as Enzo felt the pins and needles turn to daggers and blades.

Reaching the finishing line with Lilith fainting because of the cold. Cloud picked her up and put her on the bed.

"It is too early guys."

"So what are you saying?"

"I am saying that you guys have passed the tests."

"The paladin tests."

"Yes, congratulations."

Enzo looked at Lilith "Just take us home."

"Of Couse."

"I need a long bath and some shut eye."

Riding back towards the hideout, there was complete silence. Dante didn't know whether to thank him for giving them experience if they were kidnapped or left to die, or to give him a swift kick in the ass. Going home was one of the most painful journeys that Dante had even been on.

"So I hope you guys learned your lesson."

"About what?"

"The paladin training of course!" said Cloud.

"You mean," Enzo interrupted, "where you almost killed all of us three times!"

"No, silly."

"You mean we stick together no matter what." Dante said. "And trust those you know."

"Yeah."

Getting back to the hideout, Dante immediately went to sleep. Enzo wanted to check on Lilith, as he felt it was his fault that he didn't take care of her. He stayed in bed until he was satisfied that she was alright. Enzo went to Cloud.

"Cloud," Enzo asked "what is the meaning of the paladin training?"

He turned around quite pleased "You already know the answer if you are coming to me."

Enzo gripped Cloud's robe, pulling him closer. "Then don't you dare," Enzo grunted, "hurt my family."

"So you know the paladin training."

"Yeah it is to ensure that everyone survives."

"No matter what." Cloud finished his sentence.

"I am one of the last paladins left Enzo."

"So what do you want us to do?"

"In the paladin training," Cloud said "there were ten men and ten women."

"So they died?"

Cloud looked down on the floor, placing his hand on his forehead. "Yes."

"You know why but you are not telling me?"

"It was because they killed each other for that damn title, while the rest of you stuck together."

"Yes, funny enough we didn't even like each other." Cloud continued "None of the paladins in training liked anyone."

"So why the sudden change of heart?"

"We survived, we made sure that no one died out there."

"But it turned into a blood bath." As he slowly let go of his robes.

"So in the end we stuck out for each other."

"Wasn't there supposed to be one paladin?"

"Yes but sadly the people we were put up with were the best."

"So competition rose?"

"Naturally yeah. Everyone wanted to become the best."

"So I and my brother, Quinton didn't want to die."

Shocked that Enzo found out that Quinton was Cloud's brother.

"But when it all died down, we went back to the fence."

"They ordered us to kill one another."

"But you didn't!"

"None of us wanted to kill our comrades."

"So you all succeeded."

"The four of the mightiest paladins."

"What did people think?"

"They thought that we killed bears but honestly, it is who you are with and how willing you are to protect them."

"You guys will not die that easily, I keep my word on that."

"Stay strong Cloud." Enzo said, as he walked off.

He looked amazed that Enzo looked just like him and Dante looked just like Quinton. He knew that those boys would go places. Big places. He smiled and walked back to his studying room, looking at a photograph of his brother and him when they were young. He admired it so much as he remembered it was the best day of their lives. It was a picture taken with big smiles on their faces right after they survived the paladin training.

First Blood

In the training session with Enzo hitting the punching bag and Dante holding the bag, Cloud burst into the gym and said "We need to talk."

Enzo replied gasping "With what?"

"It's about fighting the ancient walkers."

Dante said "What about it?"

"Just be careful they look …" Being disrupted by a loud siren and red light flashing.

"What's that?"

Cloud said feeling scared "Oh God no. Listen to me."

Lilith busted through the door screaming "Let's get out of here!"

Cloud shouted "Follow me!"

Confused and without an explanation, they went with him as the terror on his face explained that it was serious. They kept up to speed with Cloud following him to the exit. They reached to a cross path in the base. Cloud said, "Straight ahead is where you're supposed to go."

Lilith said "What do you mean?"

"I am going to divert the attention of the walkers. They will slaughter you without warning."

"We're ready!"

"No you are not ready!" He shouted.

He ran backwards with everyone staring at him as if he was a Purple Heart solider.

Lilith turned to Enzo, grabbing and twisting his shirt and screaming "Stop him!"

"No point, he is doing this to save the world because he knows that the private military won't be enough."

Lilith stressing out, tried to chase him but Enzo caught her hand "Don't let his life go in vain."

Holding her hand, they sprinted to the door, kicked the doors open and reached the salvation of fresh air. Suddenly they saw a human outside facing behind them, it looked like a normal human until he turned around and showed his smile. Suddenly, they seemed to have got its attention by their presence. It said "You smell nice." In a sadistic tone, he showed his black eyes. Seeing this for the first time, Lilith stepped back behind Enzo and Dante came to the side of Enzo.

Frozen in fear, they didn't know what to do. Enzo tried to fight to rupture his face but it seemed that it was battle wise and managed to push him to the ground and damage his arm. Enzo quivered in pain. Dante got frustrated and charged in with full force, stalling it with a few blows to the face but it bit him, then kicked him back, grabbed his arm and flipped him over while holding his arm and dislocating it. Dante, lying down shouted "Shit!" The walker approached Lilith, she was looking left and right couldn't do anything. It grabbed Lilith by the throat and lifted her up, she was constantly punching its face to save herself and she kept trying but nothing happened. Lilith slowing dying as Enzo watched her trying to get up but she couldn't. He tried to move but the pain was excruciating. Enzo thought of Quinton dying and him being helpless and useless watching his cold corpse rot away. He shouted "Lilith!"

Suddenly, the walker was thrown to the side, due to a massive arrow stuck to the side of his arm. It left Lilith as she fell down coughing and gasping for breath while coughing out the saliva. The walker knelt down, trying to pull the arrow out from his arm but it went in too deep. Struggling to pull it out, a shadow was cast on it. Wearing all black with a hat, trench coat and trousers, a mini crossbow on his arm like a gauntlet, two daggers on his side and a massive semi-automatic crossbow on his back with ammo compiled in one shell. It shoots the bolts at ease with fast shots. An iron sights given with the limbs tucked in. The man with one hand grabbed his crossbow from his back it automatically opened its limbs with a blot cocked in and pointed at his face. The walker said "You smell nice."

"Yeah see you in hell buddy."

It showed its black eyes ready to attack him, as he shot him in the face with the bolt soaring through his face and landing on the ground with a hole left in his head. Blood pouring out of his skull and soon a puddle of velvet blood surrounding and covering his face and hair.

He picked up Lilith and said "Are you alright?"

"Help the guys please. I am fine." she said as she grasped for breath.

He helped Enzo and Dante. He said "Follow me I am going to escort you to Benjamin's base of operations."

Enzo said "Alright, who are you?"

"I am a Night walker, Demon slayer but the name is Hans."

Dante discreetly said "Alright enough chit chat let's move please!"

"Well said, our get away vehicle is close by."

They ran towards their vehicle. They got in and started strapping themselves in, Hans said "No need, I am a safe driver."

They felt less tense and unbuckled their seat belts and he started the engine. He rolled down the windows, pulled out a cigarette from his black leather coat, put it in his mouth and lit it. He reversed and throttled his way out of Cloud's base, in which he hit a barbered metal gate and rushed to the streets of the city. Driving very quickly and recklessly, dodging traffic at ease without even scraping the paint of the car. With one hand on the wheel and one hand on his cigarette, outside the window he said "The infamous blood brothers, how are you?"

Enzo screaming "I thought you said you are a safe driver?"

"I am a safe driver!"

Dante shouted "Well, we are good but can you do a bit faster."

Lilith cried, "Well he didn't crash?"

"Don't worry, you will get used to it."

Road Rage

Steering his way through the streets, Hans looked at his rear view mirror and Dante was looking at the side mirrors. Hans said calmly "We are being followed."

Dante replied "Yes, we are."

The two black jeeps following them were slowly approaching, window to window. They got clear of traffic and reached a quiet road, enough to move around. With one next to Dante and Hans, they rolled their windows down and inhaled deeply, then screamed to Hans "You smell nice." in a weird sadistic tone.

"Of course I smell nice. Its new deodorant!" Hans replied.

Hans started accelerating more and pulled out a cigarette and threw his crossbow back towards Enzo "Dante, as soon as I teleport on top of the roof of that car, I want you to take control of the wheel and Enzo shoot the other car."

"Teleport?"

"Yes, we as ancient humans have powers." he explained. "My power is smoke."

"What?" Dante said confused.

He lit his cigarette and inhaled. As soon as he exhaled, he vanished, as the smoke surrounded him. Suddenly, he was on top of the jeep's car and stuck his arm down and started shooting bolts downwards, successfully hitting the driver. As the driver lost control and headed towards the end of the bridge, he then inhaled and as the car hit the bridge and on the verge to fall, he exhaled in mid-air and suddenly vanished into thin air and landed on the passenger seat. Enzo shot the back tyre of the vehicle as it launched itself in mid-air. Enzo shot continually in mid-air so that it hit the gas pump and exploded. Embracing for cover to avoid the explosion and the car tilted away from the flames.

Hans shouted "Whooohooo."

Lilith laughing, due to not being sane as they didn't die on the road.

Driving away from the scene when they heard what they were most afraid of, the cop sirens started playing. Dante cried "Well Shit!"

Lilith asked "Aren't you going to pull over?"

"No, Logan will kill me if he knows I took his car."

Enzo, sounding surprised said "This is not even your car?"

"Nope and I don't want Logan to find out."

The cop used their speakers to communicate "Pull over the stolen vehicle."

"Well shit, I knew Logan would call the cops to screw me over."

Dante was laughing hysterically as Logan called the cops on his friend.

Hans said "Well looks like I have to change his car."

Driving the car around to dodge the cop, he saw the green light blinking and said "I am going to pass it!"

Getting closer and closer, as the signal light started blinking yellow, Dante went faster. Slowly gripping the steering wheel tighter, gently biting his lip for his need to pass the light. Otherwise, he is going to get caught by the police or die by a car crash smashing his skull or glass piercing his eyes. The light turned red and the cars slowed, passing he raced through the red light in the nick of time and managed to get out with a scrap at the back of the vehicle. The cops stopped and realised that it was pointless to pass a red light with the passing of civilian cars.

Slowing down their speed, Hans told Dante to take a right and park anywhere means necessary. They parked and Hans got out of the car and opened Dante's door, "I will drive, to clean slate this car."

They went to the auto repair shop. Parking their car inside, it was filled with people with grease on their blue tracksuits. The auto repair shop was illuminated with the colour green due to the lights. Graffiti on the walls made it look stylish.

"Fix it please." said Hans as he drove in, stepping out and throwing them the keys.

The crew of grease people went to it and started fixing it without any payments. Enzo questioned "Benjamin's company?"

"Yeah, he is really good with the government and he will clean us and this car will just be done with repairs."

Hans received a call, he picked up the phone and said "I will be there in an hour. They are fixing the car."

He ended the call saying "Okay."

The car was ready in no time, it just needed a new spray paint. Hans went in the car with all of them and said "Alright, Logan is going to kill me for ruining his car."

Lilith questioned "Who is Logan?"

"Scary guy, but he is a big man with a big heart, well that's how I see it."

They drove off without saying a word. Lilith went off to sleep, resting on Enzo's shoulder.

The Benjamin Industry

Late at night, Hans drove by the law to avoid being noticed and he didn't want any heat on him or suspicion. They landed up in the main city approaching the Benjamin buildings with a magnificent view of urban buildings. The urban city was lit with glowing lights from the lamp posts on the streets and buildings with brilliant architecture, so much so, that the lights made the buildings rather than the visual structure. They were heading to their second headquarters. It was more a building that conducted business as people, with suits entering in and out of the building or, they were outside smoking before they could enter the building. They further approached the rich architectural building. They went behind the building and the guard approached the guard as Hans parked in front of the toll gate.

"ID Hans."

"You know it's me?" He went for his pocket took out his ID and showed the guard.

"Alright, and you know what happened?"

"Yeah." Hans went quiet and didn't want to utter a word.

The toll gate opened and let Hans pass by.

Dante asked curiously "What was that all about?"

Hans immediately replied "Nothing!"

Dante placed his hand on Hans "What is it?"

He went to Logan's spot and parked it. "It's that my girlfriend waited for me outside and well I was security at that time and I let a walker through without checking ID. Blood everywhere without a body."

Lilith said "Don't worry it's not your fault."

They entered the building with Hans, it was crowded with business people. The Receptionist was busy typing, her hair was tied in a bun and she was wearing red lipstick with a white long sleeved formal shirt and a blue blazer. Hans approached her.

"There was a cold day."

"Yes."

"Get us a passage underground."

She extended her arm, reaching for a red button, under her desk and pressed it.

"The elevator is waiting for you Sir Hans."

"Thank you."

He turned to the others and said "Follow me and stay close"

Following Hans to the narrow corridor, Hans approached the janitor's room, looked left and right to make sure that the coast is clear. The room was dirty with cleaning products, brooms, mops and coats. Lilith said "You're screwing with us."

"Well, no." replied Hans.

He went and pushed the coats and pressed a red button. The room started to shake.

Enzo asked "An elevator?"

"Yep."

They went down and the door opened with a six foot seven tall man, with a slightly orange and brown beard and short hair. He had blue eyes and a great physique. He is relatively calm and has a big heart who is nice to people. When he gets angry, he is a beast with no one who can stop him. He has a deep voice and looks like a veteran in fighting the walkers.

Hans shouted "Logan!"

Logan squinted his eyes and kept staring at Hans.

Hans looked back at him and squinted.

"I could do this all day Hans."

"Okay any which way, do not take my car!"

"Anything else?"

"Why my car?"

"I lost my keys so I stole yours."

"Wow, you are a shit."

Noticing the people behind, he said "Who are these people?"

"They are in our team for judgement day."

"Hi my name is Logan." said Logan introducing himself.

Dante introduced himself along with Enzo and Lilith.

Logan said, "Well as you can see, we are the only ones left with a card up our sleeves, so we are the only hope."

"What do you mean?"

"They died in battle."

"Too many people are dying."

"Don't worry Enzo, I am here for you."

Enzo smiled a bit "That is true."

"Hans, we need to go see the boss."

"Sure."

They went towards the office and as they were walking, they saw many people on computers analysing the points in which the ancient walkers would attack. They were analysing the model figures of Hans and Logan. With their long sticks, the researchers in lab coats would point out Logan's arms and Hans' lungs as if it looked like a detective office.

They went to the office, opened the door and there was a massive deck and a big black chair behind it with a TV mounted on the side of the wall. On the other side, you can see a book shelf with hundreds of books, a rug on the floor and two chairs on the rug facing the desk. A boy roughly around 18 to 20 was writing on the paper, as they entered.

Dante shouted "You are joking?"

"Hi my name is Benjamin."

"What are you? You look 18?"

"Hey! I am your age I am a child prodigy and I finished university really early."

"So what did you call us here for?"

"Well, Benjamin Company is the company that supports the ancient war to stop all wars."

"Good luck to you guys, me and my brother are leaving, we do not want to die."

"Yeah we are not like Hans to go around teleporting."

"How could we kill them, when we have no experience?"

Benjamin immediately said "Wait, all powers are different, its ancient humans have a source of power and can go further to empower themselves, Logan and Hans are the same as you."

"What do you mean?"

"The infamous blood brothers also have powers."

"We need to find out how to get your powers but it would be different towards everyone."

"Look I do not care. I do not want to die!"

Enzo gently laid his hand on Dante's shoulder "For Quinton!"

"I am going to end this war for Quinton."

"Alright then Logan, go and give them their first experience in fighting them. I will provide expenses and research in your powers."

He turned his chair towards the window and said "Take them to the armoury and give him equipment and I know they have fighting experience but they need weapons."

"Okay Ben."

I Promise

Logan took them to the fighting grounds to show them how to attack the enemy if they were to approach them.

Lilith said "Now what?"

"We are going to the battlefield."

"I told Benjamin that we have no experience."

"Yeah, so we are giving you experience."

Hans clapped his hands to divert his attention to him "Let's get you guys weapons!"

"What is your weapon Logan?"

"Yeah we know Hans uses crossbows."

"I do not use a weapon."

Everyone besides Hans was shocked.

"You look like a tank any which way."

"He is!"

"Alright let's get you to the armoury."

"Hans, I am not coming, I am too lazy."

They went to the armoury and proceeded downwards. The lights flickered as they entered and they saw a small room with 3 walls filled with mounted weapons of heaven, it was filled with pistols, submachine guns, assault rifles, sniper rifles, swords and daggers.

"Because of ancient humans losing status to God by running away, they became more like demons. That's why guns and swords work just a good shot to their heads or hearts but that doesn't apply to them anymore but it applies to us. If it hits our hearts or heads, we cannot regenerate and die."

Lilith and everyone got closer towards the weapons, grabbing one, examining it she held a desert eagle.

Hans said "Swords and guns work on them. It hurts them, but to kill them off, you need to attack their heads or a shot to the heart, otherwise you can make them die out of blood loss."

While examining her guns, Dante and Enzo took two daggers, a sword, and five clips of ammo and desert eagle. Lilith took two of the desert eagles, Hans gave them a long black coat with a weapon holster. The black coats disguise the holster.

They got down the elevator. Logan leaning backwards, as if he was sitting on the desk said "Let us go to the road, Shall we?"

Logan tossed Hans the keys to his car "You're driving!"

Successfully catching the keys with one hand barely up, knowing he would throw the keys, they all headed to the elevator to get to the parking lot. They got into a different car, it was a black jeep. Hans rolled down the windows, pulled out a cigarette and started smoking in one hand sticking it out the window. He then held the wheel, reversed the car and went in full speed.

In the car, it was quiet until Logan pulled out his iPod. With his big hands, he flicked through his iPod and started playing trap music. Hans slowly turning his face with his eyes wide open, looking at Logan who was thrusting his head a little bit but then he started singing with Hans, slowly joining in.

Lilith said "So what's the mission brief?"

"The song is not over yet."

"Logan give her the brief."

"Fine!"

Logan reached in the glove department, inside there were seven packs of cigarette boxes and lots of documents scrambled together, he grabbed one of the documents on top and gave it to her gently. It showed pictures of people entering in and out of an abandoned warehouse in suspicion. As soon the drop hits Logan gets excited and started punching the roof of car to match the beats.

"How do you know this is a place filled with them?"

"Our inside man got us information."

"How could we kill them? There are too many."

"You got me?" Logan said with confidence.

Hans went to an alley, stopped his headlight and parked.

Hans said "Here is the plan, I will kill the guards at the front and the rest of you will go in and break shit."

"Is that really our plan?"

Logan calmly said "Well, yes of course."

"I will give a missed call when I am done with them."

Hans got out of the car and started to scout the area, it was with two guards at the entrance of the warehouse. He then proceeded to the two guards.

"Password?"

"Password, one two three."

"Wrong!"

"Your face!"

"Wrong!"

"Wait I remember, you're a bitch."

"Wrong!"

"Your death!"

"Wrong!"

He then took out his dagger in his coat, stabbed the guy in the heart, he stuck out his hand pointing towards the other guard, shot his eye and then pulled the dagger from the guard's heart.

"I was right, you did die!"

Hans gave the missed call to Logan.

"That's our queue guys, let us get in there."

The gang got out and approached Hans.

"Be careful out there guys. I know Logan will be fine but be careful, it's your first time."

"Don't worry about them, Dante has my back. Hans, watch outside for anyone coming in. Lilith, stick together, this will be a breeze."

"Don't worry Enzo, big brother is here."

Logan raised his leg, ready to kick. Hans immediately whispered "Logan subtle!"

"Okay."

He kicked the door as hard as he could, diverting so much noise, screaming with the rest of the gang behind them "What's up?" Standing, were hundreds of them. Slowly turning their heads back and seeing Logan, they said simultaneously "You smell nice."

One walker came close, looked up at him and roared at him. Looking down and seeing the walker, Logan stepped back and roared so loud that the veins in his neck started popping. His face turning red, but slightly pink, his eyes dilated and he was in a position ready to jump in hundreds. The walkers stepped back a bit and realised that he was fearful. A walker ran towards Logan, as he got closer to Logan with blood lust in his eyes and a bit of saliva on his lips and cheek drooling out of his mouth, Logan caught him by the throat, lifted him up with ease and with a single punch, he managed to kill the walker without having a chance he then choked and slammed him on the floor. Everyone looking at him in awe, the walker army got angry and started to charge forward like a stampede. Dante pulled out his sword and started running in with Logan. Enzo stuck near Lilith, mostly to protect her, rather than the plan. Logan went ramming into the walkers and as some of the walkers went down to the vigour of Logan, he eventually finished them off, cracking their skulls with a kick to the face. Dante cutting down groups of enemies with his blade, with no remorse and with a burning hatred in his eyes, thinking about the reason that his father died because of these things. He easily cut the throats of the enemies and ran them down, a beautiful execution. He sliced off their knees, as he dodged an attack from a walker by getting behind the walker and thus finishing them off by a clean cut with their heads cut off. He would otherwise stick his blade in the mouths of the enemies or easily decapitate the enemies, holding his sword with both hands. Lilith, guns blazing in the room with such accuracy was able to shoot all the enemies and reload in good pace, with Enzo behind her with a sword in his hand and a dagger in the other. Getting close, he would be able to stab them in the stomach and the dagger would be able to penetrate the neck or a good clean kill with the blow to the head with his dagger, able to get the skull. The room was in utter chaos with blood flying in the air and limbs cut off.

Outside the warehouse, with a cigarette in his hand, taking out his lighter, lighting the cigarette, taking the hit with him leaning back on the entrance of the warehouse, Hans whispered "I said subtle you retard, not brute like."

When all the noises in the warehouse had finally died down, Hans with the cigarette in his mouth almost gone, as he took his last hit, leaving it as his lips let go of the cigarette, touching the surface as his foot pressed on the floor before he opened the door and saw bodies around the four of them in a well-lit warehouse. Blood was on their hands, faces and clothes, dripping from their hair was sweat and blood and the sweet smell of victory.

"So how was your first experience?"

Dante said profoundly "I feel something."

Enzo agreed with Dante "Yeah, like as if something is surging inside of me?"

Hans immediately knew that they were getting closer to getting their new found powers.

"Alright let us go back to the lab and get your powers researched on so we could know the effect thus making you understand your power."

"Sure."

Arriving in the Benjamin Building, Hans took Dante to the lab as they were the same blood. Lilith, unaware to where Enzo had gone, as they arrived in the base. It was as if he'd vanished into thin air, but she sensed that he must have been in the medical part of the base. Walking towards where the signs showed her where to find it. Once she found the door with a red cross on, where it is visually shown where the medical supplies are, she opened the door and she saw Enzo and Enzo saw her, without his shirt. Blood on his wounds, with bite marks so deep that flesh was clearly shown and scratches showing his skin tore like paper due to the claws of the walkers. Bruises on his wounds and his face seemed untouched. The doctor came behind Lilith and passed by her, he said "Well, there is no need to be alarmed, it is something called grievous wounds Enzo."

"Ah I see doctor, that's why I wasn't able to heal?"

"Yes that seems to be the problem, you should disinfect and you will be fine, you will heal faster."

"Thank you doctor."

"Do you wish for me to do it?"

"No I will do it." Lilith said without hesitation.

"Okay well then I will have to leave I have others to attend."

He left Lilith and Enzo alone in the room. She grabbed a chair and put it in front of Enzo. She grabbed the disinfection and cloth. She folded the cloth and added the disinfection. She looked at Enzo and with her warm hands, she flinched when she was about to apply it. Enzo didn't say a word as she started to disinfect it. It started to heal much faster and the wounds started closing up. As she healed the wounds of his body.

"Thank you Lilith."

She extended her arm, with her hand as a palm and slapped him across his face. There was a moment's silence as she slapped him, as it sounded like thunder. His face turned due to the force of the slap being so hard. He left so much shame and agony. He wonder what he'd done wrong but when he looked up, he saw her face with tears in her eyes, silently crying.

"Look what you have done to me!"

Her hand extended near her face and with her wrists, she wiped her face with one hand as the other hand had the cloth. A moment's silence took place again as Enzo felt in pain and worry until he broke the silence.

"Sorry, I wasn't able to talk to you for some time because I am destined to save the world crap."

"Then Promise me you will not die."

"Why?"

"I want to go out on a date with you and you know it too."

"Yes I would love to too but you have to promise me that you won't die as well."

"I promise, because I want to see you."

"Hey Lilith, I want you to know that it was love at first sight."

"I know, I saw that in your eyes."

Thin Ice

Everyone got back to their headquarters. Dante was put into research with his shirt off. He was put in a chamber that circled him in a dark room with green lines which are squared, patterned as it went through him a couple of times. Coming out of the chamber, the researchers said "So we got a possible idea of what your powers could be like."

Everyone gathered, huddled in a circle and the scientist said "Well according to these charts, after his experience he has gotten powers mostly from his eyes."

"His eyes?"

"His eyes have the ability to manipulate time."

"How could we do that?"

"I have no idea but you could be able to slow down time and look at your options."

"Look at my options! What am I going to do, cook food really fast?"

The researcher left without saying a word with a grin on his face. He left the group without hesitation. It seemed like he wasn't able to take the puns that Dante had come up with, as he found his new found power really useless. He wanted a power like Hans, that was able to teleport him anywhere.

Lilith said "Now what?"

"I don't know, but my powers are useless."

Hans sighed "How about we go look at the board and find out what's going to happen next?"

They followed Hans into another room in which it was a board on the wall filled with pictures and locations, as if it was a detective trying to find a murderer. The board was filled with red strings connected to the pictures, to pinpoint where the leader will come out or to show its face. Hans pointed his finger to the mysterious picture in the middle of the board, where all of the red strings started distributing to the many events, to collect information and they do not know how they are collecting money to get property to start their organization.

Lilith immediately said "We were at that warehouse right?"

"Yeah?"

"What were they doing there?"

"We got a source of abnormal behaviour."

Lilith sprung out in angry due to Hans being clueless "It's because they already have money!"

"What?"

"They already have money, they worked for one of the top industries for manufacturing weapons."

"Yeah they were making weapons until we entered but for what."

"Maybe for humans."

"What do you mean?"

Logan said "It does make sense now." Dante and Enzo agreed.

"It's because the plan was not for them to destroy the world, but it was to make the humans do it for them."

"Alright, I am confused."

"How do you think all those terrorist attacks happen, wars happen? It's because they easily manipulate humans to do their dirty work."

"Yeah, you are right, that's what would make the guy above sad."

Suddenly, Dante implied "Okay how do we stop them."

"We do what we did last time."

"And what's that?"

"Destroy their operations."

"Easier said than done."

"How do you think we should do that missy?"

"What information do you have?"

Hans muttered "None."

"Well, we are screwed aren't we?"

"Alright, so let us meet the information broker and know where they are at."

"It's not that easy, we paid him a lot of money to give us the information."

"And he is a prick!" Logan shouted.

"Let's pay him a visit shall we?"

They went to a dark alley with dry paintings on the sides of the alley and trash cans on it. With dark atmosphere in the air, Hans and Lilith were the only ones there with Enzo at a sniper point, far away from them in a tall high rise building. A thin man, with a skinny like figure, very pale skin, wearing black glasses to cover up his eyes, he had short dark brown hair. Wearing a business suit and approaching the both of them, Dante and Logan created a diversion and started to create traffic. There was a lot of cars honking and yelling between different people, to make sure that no one could hear the conversation.

"Hello Hans."

He turned to Lilith "Morning there miss."

"We are not here to screw around Canute."

"So that will be 10 million please." He extended his hand giving the suitcase to them.

Lilith said "It's going to be a little different now."

"What do you mean?"

"Meaning, your life is on the line instead of the money."

He started laughing "Alright, now give me my money."

"You think I am joking?"

She pulled her phone and said "shoot something."

The glass beer glass on top of the trash can was then shot and glass pieces flew all over the place.

"Nice trick, but you came here before and played tricks to get rid of me and my love for money."

"So tell me anything you want to hit?"

He pulled out a pen "If this pen could be shot."

Placing her phone on her ear "Pen."

The pen split in two with ink flying in the air and gently landing on his thin cheeks.

"Alright the information is there." he panicked and gave the suitcase to them.

"Alright we got it Lilith!"

"Wait Hans, check the suitcase."

He opened the suitcase and found blank papers.

"We were almost coned."

Noticing that he got caught in the middle of the act, his icy cold palms got sweaty, beginning to heat up. His face got red and started to turn as red as a red tomato. Drops of sweat pouring out of his cheeks biting his lip cold lying lips, unaware to what they were going to do to him with a sniper on their back. She grabbed the suit case and threw all the papers out, while opening it.

"Give me a reason why we shouldn't kill you?"

"Okay, I tried to mug Hans but that turned really bad."

"Not good enough."

She rested her head on her phone "Right leg."

A bullet went right through his right leg unable to support to stand it went down and his left leg is supporting him as he is kneeling. Unable to hear the shots of the rifles, due to the traffic, everything was kept under the radar.

"Alright, alright please stop."

"I am giving you 10 seconds to give me the information."

"It's here!"

He reached for his pocket, inside his jacket and pulled out a sheet of paper with locations and base of operations.

She laid her head on her phone "Finish him."

"No!"

The bullet went through his head with his skull cracked and a direct hit to the brain. The blood seeping through his skull and landing on the blank papers he'd tried to con them with.

Hans said "Was it really worth it?"

"No, if he was loyal we could have kept him under our wing, but he was the same dirty walker."

"Like always."

Hans then held his hands together and prayed "Let his soul be in peace."

Lilith said "Call Benjamin's company and tell them to clean this mess."

"Sure."

"Don't worry about the gun shots, I told Logan to create noise to muffle the sound of the sniper."

They went back to their base and back to the board. They discussed about what their intentions were. Enzo said "Lilith was it right to kill him?"

"A person who has greed for money will find a way to take his revenge."

"So why kill him!"

"He would had gone to the enemy to get us."

They opened the paper and it said that their operations were fully into weapons manufacturing.

Logan shouted "Lilith was right!"

"Alright, we know their coordinations, now what?"

Everyone looked at Lilith.

"What?"

"Well, since you managed to get information and their intentions, what do you think we should do?"

"Simple, nothing!"

"What?"

"Yeah we let Benjamin do it."

"So, we let Benjamin's company take away their property."

"Yes so we will take control."

"I still don't get it, why make the humans do their work?"

Lilith smirked, "Simple, they are hunted by heaven and they are not wanted in hell and they want to make the guy above sad."

"They are lost souls?"

"Yeah."

"What about us?"

"I think we are the good guys for sure."

"Let us go to Benjamin and tell him about it."

They went to his office and saw him in his same usual seating place on his computer. They opened the door and saw there was two other people in the office. Benjamin got up and said "Sorry, but this is urgent business."

The two other business people in grey suits, got up and went left without saying a word.

Hans said "Benjamin, you need to take control of the ammunition companies."

"Are you joking? This is a chemical company, what do you want me to do, start making bombs?"

"No but the ancient humans are supplying humans to kill themselves."

"Well shit." He fell down on his chair out of exhaustion.

"I will do it, I will stop their plans to destroy us."

"Bye Benjamin, we've got much to do."

"Before you go guys" he said as he pulled out cards from his desk and gave it to Dante, Enzo and Lilith.

"Guys need to take a week off, just zip that and it will come out from our funds."

They left the place quite happy.

Lilith was a really careful girl when she was a young girl, she didn't really care about if she was a girl that she couldn't play football or hold a pistol. She was quite a different one. Once handed over to one of the paladins, she was able to learn side by side with him. From a young age, she was able to think and react faster. The paladin was convinced that her power was mysterious, he couldn't grasp the fact that she had powers or not. She had a boyfriend that she was happy with, they went out everywhere and both of them did everything together. They would go out to dinner, where he would get steak and feed the both of them. Sauce would land on her cheek and he would lean forward, moving the table a little bit, pushing his chair back with his hands clutching the table with his warm lips softly kissing her cheek and wiping it off with tissue. He would lick his lips, this would usually make Lilith laugh as she finds it stupid, funny and immature. She loved that side when he acted romantic to her. Suddenly, she wanted to surprise him by getting Cadbury chocolate for his birthday but as she opened the door, she saw another girl as she said "Can I help you?"

"Actually no."

She didn't like that her boyfriend was cheating on her with another girl and she didn't want to know why or how. She went back, crying to her father, which he knew already and as a result he cooked her favourite Shepherd's pie. She could talk to her father about anything and everything, whatever was on her mind, she would be able to tell him. He understood her pain, even as the paladins who are immune to all types of deceptions that a human would pose such as love. Paladins were strong humans, who were able to fight through the wars and some of them were strong enough to survive, but only the four of them survived in which they were financed by Benjamin's company. As they grew older, they grew weaker and unable to fight for the cause. Suddenly, he disappeared when Lilith one day couldn't find him at home. She was scared and alone until Cloud knocked down the door and found Lilith watching television. "We need to leave right now!" Cloud said. "Where is my daddy?"

"I am sorry," he said, "my best friend told me to take of you."

"What's the password?" Lilith questioned.

"Lilith is an angel."

"I will come."

Lilith and her father made sure that they had a password every time they went out and if there was an emergency that he would tell someone about the password and Lilith's foster father knew that a day would come where he would either die or disappear forever. When Cloud took her in, she rarely talked to him or even looked at him. The only question she would ask him, always at breakfast, lunch and dinner was "When is my dad coming back?" Cloud would usually turn his head away or not even talk about it. He would try to change the subject by saying "How was school?" She would usually cry, as she grew up knowing that her real father and mother left her and her foster father disappeared suddenly. Cloud would try to approach, but she wouldn't be able to talk to her. Eventually, he gave her video games to kill her time. A time came when she was big and she approached Cloud "He is dead isn't he?"

Cloud knew that it was the time for her to know that it was pointless to lie, look away or change the subject. He knew that she could take it "Actually he is missing."

"What do you mean?"

"I mean, no one could find him."

"Do you have any idea where he is?"

"Well no, he was my best friend for years," he continued "and I cannot think where he could have gone!"

He explained to her who the paladins were. They grew closer and closer, as the days past by and she understood about Cloud. Cloud explained that he was one of the mighty paladins, in which he had to stop the ancient war, around ten times. He retired early as he acquired an injury, when saving one of Benjamin's soldiers who had two kids. Paladins talk to their soldiers to keep their morale up and to make sure that even if they die, Benjamin's Company would supply the family with money or compensation, only if they have a family. Cloud took the shot of the solider in the chest. He had very bad breathing problems, but the doctors made sure that he was alright. Benjamin made sure that the paladins were needed in the war, until he realised that he was an ancient human. Only a few of them who didn't go rogue were still on the side to protect their home. Lilith found Cloud to be almost like her foster father, she knew that is always why he was his best friend.

Angry Monk

Benjamin called the full team into his office, opening the door, with Benjamin sitting down on his massive black hair, looking down at documents with papers scattered around his wooden desk, wearing his black suit as always. They got Benjamin's attention as they opened the door. Putting his documents down and his reading glasses, he looked at them with a serious face.

"Hello guys, sorry to call you at short notice."
"What happened?"
"My recon team found an ancient human."
"Wow I am so sleepy."
"And who is he?"
"He is in Tibet."
"What?"
"Yes he lives in Tibet, in which he is a monk."
"Alright, we got the good news, what's the bad news?"
"He is rumoured to have got the power of the viper's touch."
"What kind of power is that?"
"He is fast, intelligent and is very battle wise."
"So when are we going?"
"Now," Benjamin muttered "what did you say?"
"Now." Benjamin softly muttered.
"What?"
"Now." Benjamin repeated, still muttering.
"Speak up Ben."
"Right now." shouted Ben.

On the private Benjamin Jet Dante screaming "I hate you Benjamin!"
They landed in Tibet with the aeroplane landing gear wheels skidding down on the plane. They went to the airport lobby and

saw a person that held Benjamin's company's name up, he wore a black suit and tie with black shaded glasses and was bald. "We are with Benjamin's Company." Logan approached him.

"Follow me miss and gentlemen."

They followed them towards the private jeep. They entered it. They saw the thick white snow from the mountains as some of the lines are still not covered with snow. Driving towards a monastery, getting closer and closer, they caught a glimpse of it. Red paint on the walls with gold ceilings, the entrance of the monastery was painted in red and without a gate, with gold painted designs such as diamonds. Entering the building by foot, as they parked outside, as it was disrespectful to enter with the car. The monastery monk leader went in with them and told them the viper's fist is at the top of the tower. There was a massive tower that was leading upwards in a slanting line, in which the exterior was naturally painted in red.

"It is the stairway to heaven." the Monastery monk calmly said.

"Screw this" Logan shouted.

"We are climbing up." Lilith said.

They started moving upstairs, walking up with Logan slowly down panting and trying to catch his breath.

"Carry on." said Logan, panting with his hands on his knees, his body trying to support itself, as he was nearly half way there.

"Logan!" Hans turned back, extending his hand, trying to support Logan.

"Oh screw you Smoky, just go ahead and I will come back." Leaving Logan behind, they climbed to the top of the peak, there was a door. With Dante's hand grabbing the icy cold knob, turning it, thus opening the door, it was quite a dark room with candles around illuminating the small square room. With a burning smell from incense sticks burning, holding onto a wooden support with many incense sticks' ashes burned on the wooden support. Not a Tibetan or a Chinese man, but a man who is not even related to the monks or even looks like one of them. He is the same skin tone of Dante but a shade darker, he had very short hair but it looked as if he'd denied to shave himself bald. He was sitting down on the floor, legs crossed, with his hands extended, faced down and touching his knees. He faced the opposite of them with her eyes closed. He face turned slightly to the left.

"Hello strangers."

"Hello there Jonathan."

"How do you know my name?"

"I hope you know that people think of you as the fastest fighter."

"A title is just a title."

"We would like for you to fight for a cause."

"There is a cause, consequence and significance."

"We are going to fight in a war and people will die if we lose."

"War, war goes on."

"Stop talking in riddles." He pulled out his pistol and pointed at Jonathan.

The incense burns with a fiery passion thus ashes were produced. He stood up setting up new incenses.

"Stop pointing a gun at me or there will be consequences."

Hans getting slowly pissed off, pulling out a cigarette from his jacket put it to his mouth to light and started smoking it. Jonathan got angry as the smell ruined his sense of concentration. Opening his eyes, he steadily got up.

"Why smoke when I am on my path to purification?"

"Does it bug you?"

He turned facing them bowed down, within a couple of seconds the cigarette from Hans's mouth was in Jonathan's hand. He flicked the cigarette outside. Hans squinted at him, slowly pulling out another one and brought out his lighter. Jonathan grabbed his lighter and threw it out. He squinted harder as he saw his lighter being thrown out. He took it out from his mouth, extended his hand and lit it on one of the candles. "Stop it!" The monk raged.

"No!" Hans smiled.

He got angrier that his emotions were being played around with Hans.

"Now that you are not mediating, could you please talk to us?"

"Okay!" He got up slowly and proceeded to go downstairs.

After ten minutes of walking down, as they were reaching the ground level, they saw Logan sitting down on one of the steps. "I thought you said you were going to come with us?"

"I lied."

"Follow me, we will go to the tea room and talk."

They followed Jonathan into a big room with mats and pillow like seats on the floor. The room was completely wooden with windows. They were asked to remove their shoes. They sat down with Jonathan to pour tea for them.

"What is it that you want from me?"

"Well, Jonathan we want you to join us to fight the ancient humans' army."

"Why me?"

"Because you are an ancient human."

"Okay, so you know about me and my power."

"Is that a yes?"

"No, I wish to control my anger."

"Look, we are on a brink of war, people will die and blood will be shed."

"I know, I was a savage."

"Excuse me?"

"I wasn't always a monastery monk, but I was a gang member."

"A yakuza gang member?"

"Yes, I have killed and slaughtered, they called me vipers touch because I was fast."

"What made you join the monastery?"

"I don't know, I feel I went down the wrong path."

"You mean killing?"

"I killed my entire gang and people after me, they got the hint that if they tried to kill me, it was going to be a bloody battle."

The monastery leader came into the room and saw Jonathan. He bowed down to the rest of them.

"I am sorry but I overheard the conversation and I want you to take this incompetent idiot."

"What did I do now?" Jonathan sighed.

"You drink all the alcohol."

"That is not called alcohol, I can't get drunk." Jonathan said squinting.

"We have no more sake and you bring more of this American alcohol."

"Jack Daniels is good." said Jonathan, looking serious.

"You eat all the food."

"The food you give me is made for ants, I am a hungry guy."

"Get out of the monastery, you are ready for the outside."

The monks behind him started cheering and clapping behind the monk leader. Cheering as their hopes of eating food will be able to fill their stomachs and able to drink sake.

"Ah Screw you guys, I am going with them, at least they will feed me and give me alcohol." He crossed his arms and looked away, closing his eyes and his head tilted up to avoid contact.

They went to the car, Jonathan stopped them "Guys before we leave, let me just get something."

"Sure Jonathan, we are not going anywhere."

He goes to a shack where he slept in or barely slept as it was slightly lit up due to the sun shining through the gaps of the windows, as it was the only light. He would stay in, three or four nights drinking. He hated his abusive father. When he was young, he would be yelled at for being a disgraceful piece of shit. He would be called a failure when he used to try his hardest and achieved being top of his class. He wasn't able to please his father. His mother came in the way and told his father for the final time that if she found him shouting at her son for the last time, she would leave him. Thus she left him. It was just his mom and him. They were fine on their own until a day came when no one came home. It killed him trying to find her but she just seemed to have disappeared. That's when he turned to the yakuza and decided to find his path of redemption. Bloodshed in his eyes, he wasn't able to escape that past of slaughtering all those people, until the monk leader came to him and told him his path was wrong. The only thing that kept him going was a picture of his mom and him together. He picked up the picture and put it in his monk robes.

"What took you so long mate?" Dante impatiently said.

"Sorry, I was getting my equipment."

He wasn't carrying any bag on his back or a suitcase.

"So where is your luggage?"

"I got my photograph, that's the Luggage I need."

"Let us go, I do not want to argue with an idiot who mediates at the top of a mountain."

They went into the car, driving quietly with Jonathan looking back at the temple. He saw a whole different life, when he went to the plane and saw the city life. They reached the Benjamin industry. As they arrived, Jonathan was sent into the research facilities, in which they could grow and develop his powers. The researcher came out with the results, "He has a unique ability. His mind is incredible as it allows him to increase all his stats in his body thus making him faster and smarter when he strikes."

"Yes he is fast." Hans said. "Too fast."

The All Rejects

Benjamin gave them time off to cool off from all their destruction, they gave him to purify the world. Leaving Enzo behind, as he didn't want to go to the pub, as Lilith wouldn't usually go out drinking or the fact that Enzo would like to sharpen his body. The rest of them went to the pub and brought Jonathan.

"So Jonathan" Hans said. "What's your story with you joining the monks?"

"Abused as a child, shouted and beaten by my drunken father." Jonathan discreetly replied as he didn't want to talk about it. He felt shy, but he was also relieved that he'd got someone to talk to.

"Oh shit." The drinks came around with the bartender placing their drinks.

"Jack Daniels with coke for Dante."

"Jack Daniels with honey for Hans."

"A bottle for Johnny."

"And lastly one bottle of Vodka, one Bourbon," the bartender said "and a lemonade."

Jonathan looked at Logan's bottle, "Clearly, we need to have a competition?"

"And lastly bartender can I have one pink passion."

Everyone looked at Logan as he received his drink, sipping on his little pink straw. Slowly turning his head looking dead straight in their eyes of his friends not making a single emotion, and after finishing sipping on his straw he sighed with satisfaction.

"Guys, let Jonathan continue."

"So he would usually beat me with a belt or usually go out of his way to beat me for any god forsaken reason."

He started opening his drink and took a sip. He looked towards Logan, gulping down all the Vodka, as if it was natural.

"I started giving up on life," he continued "Blue and black marks on my body as I tried to cover it up before going out or to school."

"I didn't have any friends, as I was usually smart and all the girls would talk about me."

"The guys would get angry and make things worse for me."

"Then the time came, when he came home heavily drunk and beating me up with his fists."

"Blood pouring out of me through my mouth and nose."

"In the end, he told me to die."

"The next day I swear I fell and ended my life. But suddenly I woke up from my bed. Everything was the same until she came. My mom busted through the door stopping him. She died shortly after, from being over worked for me. Then again, I committed suicide but I woke up. I was supposed to die." he said. "I manage to fall in love and she knew my pain. One day she was with me and suddenly she started talking back to my father. He pulled out his belt and was about to hit her."

"Jonathan," Dante held his shoulder "you don't have to go further."

Taking a deep breath Jonathan continued, "She took the hit for me. That's when I provoked and hit him as many times as I could. I realised I was fast. Too fast. I left that remorseless abusive asshole. We went away and I was going to start university." He started to cry and i want it changed to sweat forming on his eyes, "She got a job while in university. But one day she didn't return. I waited patiently until I lost my cool. I needed answers and I contacted the police about her disappearance. Sadly they couldn't find her anywhere. The case was dropped. So that's when I joined the yakuza. They called me 'vipers touch'. I was able to kill anyone within one or two punches. Shortly, I left that life and was wanted as a hit target. Many came to kill me but I sent a message that if anyone comes for me, they will not survive for long. They took the hint."

He finished his bottle while he looked at the side where there were two finished bottles of Vodka and three black labels. Dante and Hans' glasses were piled up in a row.

Jonathan continued, "I went to the monastery to find inner peace. They gladly took me in as a shaolin warrior and a spiritual fighter and suddenly, I am in a bar with a bunch of people like me."

Logan broke the silence "Ah screw it Johnny you are alright."

"Really?"

"Yeah you can drink as much as me or Hans."

Jonathan was excited that he'd finally made some friends. He requested the bartender to play the music he'd selected. The speakers started playing trap music.

Logan got up "Holy Shit Johnny."

He started dancing in the middle of the pub and Johnny started joining him as Logan danced, amazing.

Hans started drinking down his glass. "Dante."

"Yeah Hans?"

"Remember when my girlfriend died, waiting in the parking lot?"

"Yeah."

"I killed her."

"What!"

"Only Logan and Benjamin know."

"What did you do?"

"She was an ancient human."

"So why kill her?"

"She got in control by the darkness and wanted to kill all those who opposed them."

"She started getting closer and closer." he said "She started kissing me with those black eyes."

He held his drink tightly looking down at his amber tinted alcohol, looking at his reflection and all he could see was an all-round reject in life.

"I had everything. I just wanted to marry her."

"What happened?"

"Well it was weird," he continued "I saw something."

"What was it?"

"It was darkness. Pitch Black."

"I think when she tried to put her tongue down your throat. The darkness spreads."

"Really?"

"Can't you remember something?"

"Actually thinking about it, I did see something."

"What is it?"

"A city filled with doom, death and destruction." he said "That's when I pushed her back."

"She attacked you?"

"Yeah and it got aggressive."

"She was an ancient human? What were her powers?"

"Lust."

Dante spat out his drink. Jonathan and Logan having a dance battle.

"Lust?"

"Yeah her powers were to lure enemies to her and was mostly the centre of attraction."

"And you were the one to kill them in the shadows."

"What a wombo combo?"

He chuckled "I Miss her."

"How did you kill her?"

"I don't know how it used her power."

"But?"

"I got drawn to her. I wanted her."

"But I knew that it was bad to kill my team."

"So you killed her?"

"I started pushing her back." he continued "My wrist crossbow shot her."

"Damn."

"Then on the spur of the moment, I had to complete the job. So I killed her. Her eyes were not right."

"Blood poured out her skull."

"Don't push yourself to tell me." Dante's hand placed on Hans shoulder.

"I need to tell you. You are like a brother to me."

"So blood poured out …"

"I got in a state of shock. I cried for the first time, felt sad."

"Well, it's the girl you love."

"Yeah my foster father loved his wife. He met her in college and since then, they've always been together."

"Wow."

"So I wanted to follow in his footsteps and love her."

"I loved her so much. We were together for five years. Actually ten years!"

"I was going to marry her actually."

He showed the ring on his ring finger. It was a shiny gold ring.

"I bought it three years ago, when we had our first kiss together."

"You sound like Emily and Enzo."

"Really!" Hans smiled.

"Yeah."

"I wanted to spend the rest of my life with a woman I loved."

"Didn't you have other girls before?"

"Yeah I did, but I didn't have a spark with them like I did with this girl."

"What was she like?"

"She was beautiful to me." he explained. "She wasn't the prettiest but I didn't care."

"So you liked her because she was smart?"

"Yeah I loved her because she was amazing and so sweet."

"So when did Benjamin come into the picture with you guys?"

"Well, my foster father took Logan and me to Benjamin."

"So generally you meet up with her?"

"Yeah I meet her from time to time."

"So that's how you got the money for the ring."

"Yeah that's how I got it."

"What is strange is that how did she get with the darkness?"

"Yeah it is strange she use to talk to me every time and tell me where she was."

"Sure. Unless."

"Unless what?"

"Don't get me wrong but what if she was part of the darkness?"

"What do you mean?"

"I mean, what if she already had the darkness."

"Yeah she was strange after some time."

"Strange as in?"

"After we'd kiss or make out, she would generally kiss my neck."

"And?"

"She would say, you smell good."

"Did she usually say this?"

"No, not really."

"This is getting worse and worse."

"I mean, there is a possibility that she could be a psychopathic manipulative maniac."

"Or?"

"Or she could be the right one for you." Dante smiled gracefully.

"What about you?"

"Well I haven't seen one."

"What do you mean?"

"I don't like any girl yet."

"I had a really shitty past."

"So mister hot shot what was it?"

"I had a fall out in a relationship."

"As in."

"As in, she cheated on me." he implied. "She told me to wait and wait."

"So you waited?"

"Yeah I did, but she hurt me, like burned me alive."

"So you left her?"

"Forever."

Dante started drinking, putting his hand on his shoulder "Don't worry you did the right thing."

Hans put his hand on Dante's shoulder "Well you are never a bad guy. You did the right thing."

Tu Et Brute

Dante was in the Benjamin district, exercising in the gym with water pouring out the pores of his skin. Hans and Logan went out to complete a private job for the company and took both Lilith and Enzo to give them more experience, as Dante already had enough experience of touching blades, and the company was sure that he was ready for any jobs given to him by the company. The company would not let them travel alone or let them go alone for a mission. It was either take two of them or forget the job. The contractors paid a lot for the job that Logan and the rest were on. Jonathan was in the prayer room mediating through his thoughts, as he was badly interrupted by Hans. Dante got a phone call.

"Hello Dante."

"Hello, if you want to hire me you need to talk to Benjamin's Company."

"I will give you information, if you come to me?"

"What information?" he said curiously. "Look, just speak to Benjamin's Company."

"Quinton's death!"

He sat up, Dante's heart started beating faster, gripping his phone harder, flexing his muscle as his veins were popping out. Clutching his fist, his short nails stabbing himself, shifting his head a little bit to the right, pressing the phone closer to his ear to make sure that he received the right information and he is hearing the right stuff.

"What about his death?"

"I know why, I know who, I know where, I know everything."

"Who are you?" Dante said, with anger in his voice.

"Meet me, I will give you directions."

The call ended without another word. Dante didn't think for a minute, if it was a trap or if it was real. He wanted to know the reason he wanted revenge. The more he thought of it, the more he wanted someone's blood. If he was unable to get a name, he was convinced that he would destroy the full world to make sure that one guy died.

The next day Dante got another phone call. Picking up the phone, skipping the courtesy of any conversation, the caller said, "Get out of the building."

He dressed up heading out of the Benjamin industry. The night was young, the stars were shining brightly in the night, with the only source of light being the lamp posts or lights from the urban city.

"Go across the street."

Following the instructions of the mysterious phone caller, he did so.

"Turn into the alley."

He turned into the alley.

"Finally, I wish for you to die!"

Dante, on the spur of the moment, sharply turned behind him, blocking the knife but unable to see the attacker's face. He dropped the knife to the other hand. Dante cleverly foreshadowed the action, thus breaking out of the defensive shell, turned around and got into a defensive stance. He hid his face from the shadows.

"Who are you?" he yelled, "Why do you want me to die?"

"You are a very important person."

"What do you mean?"

"I mean you are someone that has great power."

"I am not here to play your damn games." Dante yelled. "I am here for Quinton."

"Oh you mean the guy who died at St. John the Baptist church."

Dante looked shocked, confused and angry.

"He died by a log almost closing at his heart." He continued "The four other priests were cut open, obliterated with limbs everywhere."

Dante fell with his knees on the floor, arms flailing, slowly trying to search for the meaning of all of this. Confused as his brain was scattered to how he could acquire delicate information.

He crossed his arms as he took a step ahead. His black blazer, white inner shirt, black trousers and shiny black shoes were shown with leather tight gloves.

"You want to know who killed your dear old dad?" he yelled. "It was me."

Out of rage, he screamed with his left eye blinking a yellowish like color rapidly, as he saw the events. Out of desperation, of the situation getting out of control, he pulled out his silver desert eagle pistol with a silencer attached and shot the bullet at him. Dante fell down, craving death as he knew he was the reason that Quinton died.

The man shot again, but suddenly the bullet was caught by Jonathan. He threw the bullet on the ground.

"Viper's touch."

"Who are you?" Jonathan said "You know who I am."

"I know a lot of things. I am an information broker."

The bullet pulled out of Dante's wound and started healing. Dante slowly got up.

"I will tell you once more, before I kill you." he yelled "What is your damn name?"

"Search me up on Benjamin industries." He continued "They call me the Shade."

He walked away into the darkness until they were unable to see him.

"How did you find me Jonathan?"

"I got a sense of danger from you. I spoke to Benjamin, thus checking the cameras."

"So you followed me here."

"Yes. I knew you were in danger."

"Thanks!"

"Any which way, let's tell Benjamin about shade."

They went back into Benjamin's office. He was wearing his business suit, talking on the phone with someone. Dante kicked the door open on the spur at the moment.

"Oh my God Dante! I may be rich, but a door costs money!" Benjamin yelled.

"Who is shade?"

There was a brief moment of silence. Benjamin started sweating. His face was getting red, he turned it away from Dante, trying to conceal the fact that his knowledge would make Dante angry. He didn't want to say a word. He tried to change the topic up to the point Dante got even angrier.

"Who the hell is he?" he yelled. "I almost got killed."

He slammed his hands on Ben's desk, looking into his eyes and he went much closer to his face. Ben saw from his face that it was either, he spits out the information or Dante would beat it out of him.

"I can't Dante!"

"Don't make me go there." Dante fearfully responded, "I will beat it out of you."

"Sorry but I will take the hits."

He grabbed his desk from the side, the veins from his hands clear as emeralds with his eyes widened like that of a tiger. He threw the table to the side and as he threw it, papers flew into the air with broken pencils, spilt ink and broken pens on the floor. Benjamin didn't wear any trousers as he was only in his boxers.

"Wow look what you have done? You know my secret."

Dante was unable to laugh.

"Okay Dante if you really want to know who he is?"

"Yes."

Then Logan came into the destroyed room.

"What happened in here?"

"Logan, go call the rest of the team."

Logan looked at his face and looked at his tiny boxers which had hearts on them.

"Okay." He said slowly, yet confused.

"Shade is the name of my former employer," he explained. "He was one of the most successful highly paid in the company."

"How much?"

"Around 2 million for a job."

"What?"

"Yeah and that's for a small job such as pick up and drop off a package."

"Suddenly, he became more rogue," he sighed "and left!"

"Why did he leave?"

"I don't know, his intentions were not with me."

Dante stood up "He killed Quinton and the other priests."

"Dante let us not jump to conclusions!"

"He told me!"

"He is one of the best assassins. It is their job to manipulate or deceive you."

"I am with Dante with on this one." angered Enzo. "Either I will kill him or he will."

"What is his real name?"

"His real name is Lazaro Dewitt."

"He is an ancient human." Jonathan said.

"He is right?"

"Yes and to make it worse," Ben explained, "his power is deception."

"What type of power is that?"

"It is quite different."

"He is able to go invisible before the naked eye, also having the gift of tongues."

"Gift of tongues?"

"Never engage in a conversation with him."

Benjamin looked at everyone with a serious face, "Don't ever negotiate with him."

"Benjamin what are you trying to say?" Logan screamed. "Why are you telling us now?"

Dante stopped Logan "Logan, let him finish before we come to conclusions."

"Oh you're mister nice guy? You trashed his office!"

"That is what I mean, by don't negotiate with him."

"What do you mean?"

"His power will deceive you" he calmly said. "Wonder why he is the greatest assassin?"

"Why?"

"He doesn't kill the targets. He brainwashes the other targets to kill for him."

"So he doesn't kill, he gets someone close to kill the target for him?"

"Yes."

"I don't get it." Enzo whispered.

"What happened?"

"I mean, how could a paladin lose?" Enzo questioned. "I mean he is one of the smartest humans isn't he?"

"No."

"Benjamin, what is Quinton?"

"He is the oldest ancient human."

"Oldest? You mean …"

"Yes, when your father was alive."

"What the hell!" Enzo yelled. "You took so long to tell us!"

"Well, Quinton died by someone he couldn't kill." Benjamin explained "By someone he couldn't even touch."

Enzo stood up and looked at Dante with eyes of fear going back slowly. He tripped on the floor, landed on his arse, pointing his finger, shaking and trembling in fear. He knew he was the only one, as Enzo was in college just graduated the only person who was close to him the only one who was close to his heart and close to him in person around that time.

"You." He whispered "You killed him."

Dante twisting his head slighting looking down denying that he did it.

"No." Dante placed his hands on his head screaming as flash backs came back into his mind.

He drove to back to Quinton with shade in the car. He got out of the car, killed Quinton with nothing in his eyes but regret that he couldn't stop Dante from shade. That's why he said he was sorry specifically to Dante. He saw him set up the scene as Lazaro did all the dirty work. He then got in the car with Lazaro walking out, getting out of the car and walking away into the distance, from the church. As a result, Dante picked up Enzo a little late, carrying a pack of beers for Enzo to congratulate him. It was a trick.

Dante came back from the flashback and stopped screaming. There was a moments silence, Benjamin pushed him to the ground, restraining his arms.

"Benjamin what are you doing?" Lilith yelled.

"Quickly restrain him!"

Logan caught Dante by arm with one leg and Hans by another.

Enzo pulled out a gun from his coat and pointed at Benjamin "What are you doing!"

"He will commit suicide after the job is done."

"It is one of the tricks Lazaro pulls. It is quite clever as there would be no evidence."

Logan pulled Dante up, restraining him. Lilith walked up to him and slapped him.

"Damn." Enzo said.

Dante came back to his senses. "Guys?"

"Let him go, he's back."

Logan, let go.

"It was me wasn't it?" Dante said, welling up.

"Dante." Lilith whispered.

"Enzo I am so sorry."

"Hey brother, at least you are alive."

"Hey Ben, I got a question."

"Yeah."

"What were Quinton's powers."

"As great as your fathers."

"So you mean …"

"Your father's was the Eye of the world," Ben explained. "Quinton's power was deception."

He hit the floor as hard as he could.

"Hey" Logan said, "Don't worry about it."

"I don't understand."

"I mean, we are behind you. We are with you all the way."

A shady past

Walking through the crowd of people, Lazaro looked down, hating each sight of every human being he saw. He looked at each and every one of them, thinking how disgusting each human was. He always disliked the sight of humans, he never really liked them from the start. He knew that his father and mother were not there for him and were trusted on other people but the humans treated Lazaro like shit. Everywhere he went, he was ill-treated. He remembered school life, as he could never forget, mostly students referred to him as an awful, atrocious and gross guy as he didn't like life and usually liked songs such as punk or rock. He would listen to those songs, as it would give him courage to fight everyday school life, as he only got songs that conveyed a meaning towards him. He would be able to dress up as he didn't like being mocked. He dressed as if he was a depressed person, as they already made fun of how depressing and violent his music was anyway. He wore the same clothes, like any person, as he was a fun person and a creative one. He was mocked since he had no father and mother, he was taken in by a very wealthy farmer. Lazaro didn't like anyone besides himself. Passing through his life, he bumped into a girl and fell over with all his books and test papers on the floor. He didn't want to show his test papers to anyone, as he knew he would be called a nerd. Picking up his papers as quickly as he could, without even looking at the girl he bumped into, he quickly ran into his class but he'd left a paper behind. The girl saw that on his paper, he'd got a B. The girl gave it to him in his next lesson. He took it, looking down, not even trying to show her his bright blue eyes. He was awfully shy and didn't like it when women stared at his eyes. She suddenly went closer with her soft hands, gently touching his sharp chin slightly giving it a slight push as she went incredibly close, examining his eyes. He blushed so much that he looked like a red tomato. She went back and handed out his test paper and he whispered "Thank you."

Faintly, but she surely heard him. She went close to his ear, pushing her luscious blonde hair behind her ear "You're not too bad yourself." She whispered.

His heart for the first time, started beating when she spoke those words to him. No one had spoken to him in such kind words before he left. It was as if maybe his faith in humanity had restored itself. Skipping back home, was actually one of the weirdest moments, as he would usually not think of any girl until it hurts him.

She went with Lazaro after classes and he started to help her with her studies, especially with her math. She grew fond of him, she started to love him more and more when they talked, joked or even smiled together. She would tell him about her problems in her small world and how guys kept following her. It would demoralize him, but he wouldn't give up as she'd already told him that she was all he needed. For the first time, he felt the need not to kill himself or a day where his life wasn't pathetic or insufficient than it is to an ant. For some reason though, he felt that maybe his heart might be tortured by an unexpected surprise.

He went into class with a couple of guys, when getting up walking towards him were three of his most hated bullies. They gripped his shirt and lifted him up. Buttons started to tear off and his clothes started ripping as they lifted him up the wall. Afraid at what might happen, he started asking questions "How do you know her?"

"When did you see her?"

He didn't want to say a word, he was ready for his first fight and his loss in a fight, just thinking about her. She ran into the room screaming "Stop!" he ignored her and placed his hand around his skinny neck, choking him. Panic broke out, as she started hitting him telling him to stop it. Getting blacker around his eyes, thinking how it had got this bad. Questions came into his mind, starting with, why me? Why do bad things happen to me? Why do bad things happen to good people? They threw him to the ground and started stomping and kicking him until he felt satisfied. Trying to pull him away, she grabbed him, pulling him. Lazaro went into a turtle stance, being on the defensive. Managing to cool him down, she went to Lazaro "I cannot see you after class."

His heart broke as he looked at her. She placed her hand at his face, rubbing his cheek to his chin. "I love you!" His heart broke in two.

After school he saw her in a corner, as he forcefully tried to lay his hands on her, trying to take her. He knew from the moment he saw that guy placing his hands on her, he'd get really angry. Fury burned inside of him, his blood boiling as he knew that he would never be able to do anything but he tried to stop her, he went up to him and said "Back off!" She told him "Go, we will be fine."

He walked along that same highway, towards home, it seemed duller than before. Lying in bed before trying to get some sleep, his mind was clouded with haze. "Go, we will be fine." He didn't like it, what was his reward for running away? Better that than to see tears in her eyes, as he shouted at her. She had protected him up until that fateful day, when he was caught by the same bullies. He'd never known a love so strong, that it could never be rivalled at. He saw his aftermath was tears in her eyes as he saw a black eye on her. He knew that he had to avoid her. Every time they made eye contact across the hallway, he had to turn away and say to himself, it was for the best. He knew deep down that if he were to talk to her again, that either she would get hit at or he would get in trouble and she would have to come in to save the day, but in the end still get abused by her forceful boyfriend. She was scared to let go of him as she feared that she would get abused to a limit that she could not take ending her miserable life. The same bastard who abuses her went up to him "That black eye was the best moment of my life." Enraged, irritated and offended he got on the offensive. He couldn't stop him.

Suddenly his anger evoked his potential to kill. He noticed that he was able to persuade anyone by talking into them and planting the most dangerous memories inside of them. He knew that it was time to destroy that man that hurt the only lover that he desired. The next day he started to use it on him. But what he unleashed was devastating. He made the guy go into a nightmare terror, that he saw his abusive father beating his mother and later on beating him. It made him go insane with his mind ruptured, he was able to go for the woman he fell in love with but he saw the fear in her eyes as she saw what he was capable of. She cried "Stay away monster."

He looked towards the guy he resented on the floor covering his face on the floor, covering his head, trying keep him safe from his father pouring his eyes out. He saw the destruction he had caused and she saw it as well, that his powers to deceive the mind and the eyes of his opponents was one of the most powerful and he spoilt it for his revenge on those who he thought unworthy of a world. He knew good things happened to bad people and he knew bad things happened to good people. He looked at the shiny reflection of himself and he saw himself as she saw him. A monster. He tried to walk forward "Listen." But she quickly responded "Get back away from me you demon."

He stepped back looking down, putting a hood over his face, turned around trying to conceal his tears. For his first love and his first heartache, he knew this heartache would never end. It rained while he was coming home. He removed the hoodie in the rain, letting the raindrops hit his head His hair straightened due to the cold wet rain. Reaching home, he knew that he had to leave. After he graduated, he hugged his only friend, his only caretaker and his only father that he knew. He was glad he never committed suicide every time he went on the roof top though he wanted to, but he thought there was a purpose in life somewhere, he just needed to find it. He found out, when he was working for a company that the boss found out about his powers. It was in competition with Benjamin co-operation. He started to nurture his new found power. The wealthy company owner knew that he would make a fine hitman. He made him do jobs that were particularly dangerous. He worked inside Benjamin co-operation and made sure that he was a spy to deliver information back to him. But it wasn't as useful as he'd hoped and Lazaro began to like Benjamin and knew he didn't want to destroy his future. He started to take on hit jobs by easily getting close to those who hurt other innocent humans. He considered them worse than scum. He looked at them and knew that he had to get to someone he trusted. He would usually like to go for his most favourite tactic which was get the closest person to like him and kill him. He would like to get up close with the target's most trusted right hand man, in which he would try to judge whether the man should die or not. He heard a lot of cases in which the people had supported wars for money. Sold drugs to men, women and even children whenever Lazaro heard that he knew that they needed to die, whether it was for the better or for the worse, he hated it when innocent children got involved. He heard worse and worse. At the end of hearing their blood soaked story of killing, slaughtering and even doing wrong in society, he would then charm them by the way he talked. Getting hypnotized by the way he said his words, his victim goes to his target and assassinated them for him. He felt that he wasn't responsible and he would never be connected if the police, FBI or even the pentagon got involved. He would love to see the eyes of the victim, when he was stabbed by the one he trusted. He couldn't think of a better way. He became really famous and people started to call him by a nickname to suit his identity which was Shade. He loved his name and he was getting really famous. No one would know who Shade really was, only a handful of people would know his name, he had one of many, such as Shadow Warrior or Black Assassin. He would usually like to take long strolls in the park. He would eventually like to disappear in front of people. From time to time, he would check up on the girl he used to love. In the shadows, as the waiter would come in with flowers giving it to her while she sat down in a restaurant trying to have meal after her busy day. He would constantly watch her. He didn't want to see a scar on that pretty face. Every time he saw her, he always wanted to say hi again and try again whether she knew him or not. He soon learned to understand that he was an ancient human that was in the midst of an ancient war that was brought upon him. He was more of a solo guy and didn't usually like to talk or take orders from anyone. He would just want the slip of who to assassinate, in which he would be able to earn around 1.2 million for each hit to assassinate one of many wealthy people in the world. He didn't care if it affected other people. He just cared about that girl. Whenever he saw her with financial problems, he would dig into his long black coat, in which he would find much more money that he would usually find. He would knock on the door with the letter slipped under her door. He would disappear above the building where he could see her from his mansion, with his binoculars, he would smile a bit and think that what he did was right.

He remembered Quinton that he had found his only father but he found that he was his actual father. He raced there thinking what his father was going to look like. Just as he was about to knock on the door, he wanted to get a glimpse of his father. Surprised that his father had moved on, that it touched his heart. He was moved that his father had taken care of boys around his age, but he was also sceptical about himself. Hatred grew inside him as he left racing away. But Quinton saw his son through his window, as only Quinton would like to peek in his surprises, as he tends to get too excited that he just wants to take a peek and act surprised, just like when Enzo and Dante tried to surprise him.

Lazaro had to keep a watch on, those two people, he knew his mistake for leaving the only girl he loved behind and he had to take care of her no matter what. He had to make sure that Quinton was safe and sound.

But in the end he remembered that all humans are scum, most humans treat one another badly and start to curse or beat up other people for the good or for the bad. He mostly took up jobs where he could use the best tactic he knew, to eliminate those who he sees unfit to be part of the earth. He made a lot of sacrifices. He knew that the sum of the earth must die, whoever he sees that must die, he likes to hear the cries in vein. But in the end he knew that humans were scum, even if good people are effected, whether children were involved, someone must have put them in that place. Someone around them must have had bad company that got them involved with drugs. In wars there are two sides that uses people to kill one another.

He bumped into an old lady as her purse fell down with all her belongings on the ground, her lip balm, her purse and her wallet. He helped her pick it up as he tried to put blind eyed but she placed her hand at her back with her veins popping out trying so hard to kneel down. He didn't want to help but he went down with his coat hitting the ground. Picking up her items and placing it back in the bag. Giving the bag to her "Your bag ma'am."

"Thank you, you are such a gentleman."
"But ma'am?"
"Yes?"
"I would like my wallet back." as Lazaro looked at her and smiled.
"Oh dear, I am not a thief sweetie."
"Listen to me you old hag," Lazaro whispered "give me my wallet or else."
"What are you going to do?" she said "Look at the people around you!"
"You are stealing from the wrong guy."

Lazaro had some morals, he will not use his powers on people who are significantly weak. He'd stuck to that rule ever since he stopped that guy who abused the girl he loved.

She decided to make a run for it with his wallet. He watched, as she ran right past him through the crowd. Suddenly, she bumped into him again, she looked down and saw a blade in her and she looked down and saw the blood staining her clothes spreading like a virus. He peeped his head near her ear.

"No one is watching you old hag." he said "People like you are worse than shit."

He reached in her coat and grabbed his wallet. He walked into the shadows, sticking to his judgement of people whether they are young, married or even old, he hated the world and he whispered to himself, humans are disgusting.

Wicked Game

Smoking outside, Hans holding his cigarette in one hand and in the other his phone, checking his contracts and his money he'd collected. As the cigarette burnt, he got frustrated by it and threw it. He bought a wooden pipe which was curved nicely with a dragon's claw, clutching the end of the pipe where you put the tobacco. He pulled out his tobacco and tossed it inside, he would light it with his favourite zip lighter engraved 'Lady killer'. He would keep it close to him, always, as it reminded him of her as she gifted it to him for their first mission. He would usually like to be alone and smoke, but if it was around his gang, he really didn't care, he found them like brothers. If anyone would have died he would have gone on a killing spree but he knew that wouldn't happen. As immortals, he knew that they wouldn't die easily. He chuckled a bit, remembering the first time he smoked was when he was young, a group of guys threatened to kill him unless he smoked a cigarette. Eventually, to save his life, he did it. The police came and arrested the young group, taking Hans home. He went home and saw his foster father, in which he found out later, that he was one of the four mighty paladins. He knew he smoked, but he couldn't blame him or scold him as he knew that Hans was immortal. He usually caught him smoking, but he really didn't care as in the end, he knew that he wouldn't die and leave him. Hans soon learnt how to teleport. When he got bullied in school, they would call him names because he smoked, but most girls found him hot and irresistible. Once they got him surrounded while he was smoking, he just moved out and teleported. He got an idea and started to move around whilst punching them. Hans remembered how he met Logan for the first time.

Logan was a stray, he was a big child and no one wanted to play with him, as he was unusually tall for his height and was mostly shy. He was usually scared of the dark and didn't have any friends as his face was scary but he felt really lonely. He used to get bullied a lot. They used to make him go in the closest in the dark and make him stay there. Crying in the dark until the caretaker came and scolded the bullies and made them get out of Logan's room. She stayed in the room with Logan and made him strong. "Logan if you stop crying in the dark, I will give you cookies and milk."

Logan stopped crying, wiping all his tears with his soft little hands, he looked straight as if he was staring death in the face and stopped crying. She opened the door and she hugged him. "Good job Logan." she whispered "I am so proud of you."

Eating his cookies and milk, he saw Hans across the table with Hans' foster father and the caretaker standing at the door. "Logan this is your new family." she said. "Be nice and be strong."

He kept those words at heart and that is how he is indestructible, like a tank.

Smoking his pipe, he remembered his girlfriend. He only smoked cigarettes because she would like to smoke cigarettes instead of pipes. He emptied his smoking pipe by slightly whacking the ash from the pipe. He cleaned it with a small square cloth that is usually used for cleaning glasses. Suddenly his phone rang. He knew that he was off duty and that they would have to pay him extra or he would decline the job easily. He was usually smart enough to hear out the offer before declining it. He picked up his phone and gently placed it in his ear. "Hello," he said "if you have any enquires about hiring me, I am on my day off so you can choose to pay me extra or I decline it, but I will hear it out."

"Sure, how about killing your future." she said.

"This discussion is over." he said calmly.

"Wait." she said "Hans!" Just as he was about to end the call, he heard his name.

"You know my name?" he said. "Either you know me or you've contacted me before."

"Meet me around five in the afternoon." she cried. "Don't be late."

"Hey? Are you crying?"

Hans generally hates crying women. He was a big softy for women who cry. He cannot stand himself for seeing a woman cry or being sad, he would try every possible action to make sure that she was either happy or at least not crying.

"Fine, I will arrive there." he said "Where is it?"

"The parking lot."

"What, you mean the parking lot in the Benjamin building?"

"Yes."

"Okay."

Hans ended the call being suspicious in mind. He went to the armoury first and equipped himself with his writ bow and two daggers, just in case it was an ambush.

In the elevator going down, sheathing in his daggers and hiding his wrist crossbow in his long coat, as the elevator arrived downstairs, he felt something was wrong. He looked around and became nostalgic, as if he'd seen this place before. He looked left and right, slowly walking ahead, until Rose, Hans' girlfriend came with the dress to surprise him. She had glowing blue eyes, red velvet hair and pink lips. Hans would love those pink lips and usually she would apply pink to make them glow for him. Stuck in time as he saw her. Tears forming, falling down from his eyes, running down his cheek. She wore his favourite dress, which was black with white poker dots. He felt sick, very sick and started coughing a lot. A car from the parking lot, Hans knew it was his. "No" he yelled "No, stop."

She went to him and hugged him "Stop Rose, come here."

He wasn't able to move, he just saw the horror in his eyes and he saw himself kill Rose. Hans screamed "No". He saw the blot stuck to her as he ran towards her skidding on his knees to a stop and picked her up. Crying over his mistake, he didn't see those blue eyes, all he saw was those obsidian black eyes.

The illusion ended, Hans saw the outside guard's body in his hands as it was covered in blood. He placed the guard on the floor and saw his hands blood red.

"You do miss me?"

Hans turned around slowly trying to conceal the wetness from his cheeks. He wanted to know if she was alive or if she was dead. He wanted answers, he wanted to know what was happening in this ever breaking world. Reaching to a point where he turned around fully and he saw her with that poker dot dress with those blue eyes. "Who are you?" Hans questioned "What are you?"

"Hans it's me, Rose." she said, walking towards him. "This time it is not an illusion."

"I've got so many questions."

"I know."

"But I want you to answer my first questions!" Hans demanded.

"I am an ancient human hybrid."

"What?"

"I am an ancient human and a lesser demon."

Hans fell down to his knees "How did this happen?"

"I was always like this. I was different."

"What do you mean?" He yelled. "Why are you a demon? What the hell is happening?"

"As an ancient human you are forsaken by both sides." she implied "From good and evil."

"I know we are hunted by heaven and hated by hell and unaccepted by purgatory."

"So I went to both sides and came back."

Hans backed off a bit, getting away from her. "I don't know how to feel?"

"Aren't you happy?"

"No I am definitely not happy." Hans yelled.

"Why?" she started to cry. "Why aren't you happy?" She tried to come closer and closer to comfort him but the more she came closer the more he stepped back, until she realised, he was scared of her and couldn't believe that she was something like that.

"Hans, you are breaking my heart."

"Rose," Hans couldn't speak due to shock "you broke my heart."

"No, I didn't mean it."

"Where were you?" Hans said "Why now?"

"I was fighting in purgatory, they wouldn't let me come out to Earth."

"And?"

"It was hard for me." walking closer to Hans "Hans please."

"No!" he yelled "Get back."

"I wanted you so much." she cried "I did all of this for you."

"You made the wrong choice."

"If you won't come with me," she cried "I will force you."

She tried to use lust on him as. She placed her palm on her lips and blew a kiss to him. Hans stood straight, as her power hit him, he was unaffected but he went closer, he grabbed her and kissed her.

"No." Hans whispered "It's not the same."

"Wait what?" Rose said, confused.

"I am not under your spell."

Lilith came down the elevator. Rose saw Lilith "Who is she Hans?" she looked at him with anger in her eyes.

"Hans, who is she?" Lilith questioned.

Rose approached her. "Who is she?"

Enzo came down the elevator. "What the hell is a demon doing in our base?" He pulled out his gun and pointed at her.

"Everyone back off." Hans yelled.

"Hans, what is happening?"

"Guys." he said with disappointment "This is Rose, my dead fiancé."

"What?"

"Spare me the details." Hans said "Please."

Logan came down with the keys in his hands. He looked forwards and saw Hans with Rose. Hans fell down on the floor. "What the hell is happening?"

Logan sprinted and grabbed Hans' skinny body and got him here. "Don't worry Hans I got you."

"Um. Logan I am fine."

"Shut up."

He brought out holy water and threw it at her with the lid closed.

"Holy shit I didn't open the bottle."

His palm smacked his forehead.

"Enzo get your ass over here." He dragged Lilith and Enzo towards Logan.

"Hans, explain what is happening?"

"Wait." Hans said.

"How did you escape purgatory?"

"I made a deal with the gate keeper of purgatory."

"What was the deal?"

"That I would come in and out of purgatory."

"But?"

"But I had to pick a side."

"Hans, look we are on a mission."

"Go for it Logan."

Logan went to the car and went for the mission with both Enzo and Lilith.

Hans said "Rose are you here because of me?"

"Yes!"

"Get out of this place."

"If I see you again, I will kill you."

"I know you hate demons and I am sorry but I had no choice."

"You know that my father died to demons."

"I had no choice, please just trust me."

"The next time we meet, it will be on the battlefield." Hans' eyes were deadly serious "And we will not be allies."

"Bye Hans."

She left him alone. He felt depressed that she is the thing he hates, but he still loved her.

Angel Reincarnation

They managed to skive off some days as Benjamin prepared the next course of action. Enzo was dedicated to asking Lilith on a date before the worst happened. Getting to her dorm inside the Benjamin Building at the top floor, in which the richest companies enjoy a night while discussing deals with him, and five rooms were always occupied. It was well lit with windows covering the end of the corridor with sunlight coming through or you could gaze at the night. It was sunny outside, as it was somewhere around morning. He whispered to himself on how he was going to ask her out and rehearsed all his lines, while slowly walking to her dorm. He arrived at her dorm, his arms were sweaty as it was warm outside and he was nervous that she might reject him for not talking to her for a long time. Being nervous won't help him. His warm fingers pressed the cold doorbell, waiting for a couple of seconds as she said "Coming!"

She opened the door with excitement in her eyes and a smile that nearly killed Enzo by melting his heart. "Hi Enzo."

"Hey Lilith."

"What happened?"

"Nothing, I just wanted to talk to you. It's been so long since we last talked."

"Yeah it kind of has."

"Look I want to talk and if you're free …"

Her eyes started dilating as she tried to contain her excitement in trying to reach out to Enzo and so was he reaching out to her. Enzo's heart beating rapidly, his cheeks getting red and making it hard to talk to express himself, in a way that she would accept him. He didn't want any other girl to hold him except her.

"I was thinking if you are free, would you like to go out with me?"

"When?"

"Now if possible?"

"Okay, I will call you."

She kept smiling towards the end, with Enzo's heart pounding as she closed the door. He skipped along towards his dorm across the hall.

Thinking about what to wear in the summer time. A mixture of feelings sprung inside of him, he describe. He was mostly happy and excited but he felt pain as well, knowing that he wasn't there for the one he previously loved but now knowing he has the power to protect her. He feels a little better knowing that he feels he can protect her. He wore normal clothes, like a white shirt and white short trousers and a straw hat, he didn't want to over dress for her. She messaged him saying 'Come outside my door I will be out in a second'. Enzo got his card and phone in his pocket, he rushed out of his door and waited outside for a minute. She opened the door and she was an angel in disguise. He was empowered by her brilliant aura. She wore a white summer dress with poker dots on it. Her silky black hair tied in a ponytail while, her glowing blue eyes stunned him. Looking at her, he felt like the luckiest person alive, to have her with him. She extended her hand waiting for Enzo to hold her hand. He reached out and held her soft warm skin and gently held her hand, looking at her eyes as she looked at him with passion colliding in their eyes, as he pressed the elevator button heading down. She said "Where to?"

"Where do you want to go?" he replied.

"I want to go for coffee and cake."

"Sure, I know just the place." he smiled with glee.

The red carpeted walls of the elevator with a yellow light emitting from the elevator lights hit Lilith's skin emitting a kind of glow which attracted Enzo. Holding her hand a bit more tightly, she turned her head, paying attention to him looking at her eyes. If he saw tears in those eyes, he would break down and cry. He moved slightly closer to her. She noticed his shyness and tried to move forward with him. From the 15th floor, going down was longest time they'd ever waited, getting lost in each other's eyes, without saying a word to each other. Finally, they reached ground floor reception, with business people walking around not paying attention to how different Enzo and Lilith were.

Lilith said "I think we should walk."

"Of course."

They went out of the building and walked together, holding each other's hands. Enzo got a sense that he was being watched by someone.

"What's wrong?" Lilith asked.

"Nothing, I just feel as if were being watched."

"Don't worry about it, I think it is just your brother looking out for his baby brother."

"No, it can't be, all three of them went to the party with Benjamin."

"Why didn't you go?"

"I wanted to spend some time with you, of course."

Ignoring all signs of possible danger, he thought that the only thing that could make his day better was for Lilith to understand that he loves her and would do anything to be with her. They arrived at the coffee shop's glass door. It had yellow walls and was filled with lots of people, drinking coffee and eating cake. With quiet conversations, the atmosphere was quiet with the sweet aroma of coffee in the air. It was relaxing, they went to the counter, Enzo said "So what cake do you want?"

"Cheesecake with strawberry syrup." Lilith replied.

"What?"

"I said I wanted tiramisu."

Enzo became vigilant and knew there was something wrong here. It wasn't the shop, it was someone watching him.

He looked at the shop assistant "Two tiramisus and lattes please."

He purchased and sat down.

"Lilith I do not feel so well."

"Do you want to leave?"

"No I mean, I feel there is something wrong."

"Don't worry about it."

"I will be right back."

Lilith went to the toilet. As she left, the cake arrived. Looking down with his hand wrapped around his stomach and his other arm on the edge of the table supporting his head, Enzo was feeling insecure. He couldn't tell if it was butterflies in his stomach or a revolting feeling in him, making him nauseous. His hands were starting to get numb and he was getting goose bumps.

"I'm back."

Hearing her voice was a light in the darkness and it was the cure for his nausea. Looking up, his eyes deceived him. He saw another woman who was pale in skin colour with curly hair and green eyes wearing the same dress as Lilith holding the cheesecake with strawberry syrup. He whispered "Emily?" The fear in his eyes pierced his heart, as it went in flames and his vision was getting blurry. His hands were shaking and his ears started ringing. He got up violently.

"Are you alright?"

He started to rub his eyes and saw Lilith at the same spot with the same dress. He looked outside the window and saw Emily outside staring at him. Lilith gazed at Enzo and looked outside and saw the woman wearing white robes outside the shop staring at Enzo. Unable to say anything, he grabbed Lilith's hand and ran out of the shop.

Lilith running with Enzo, she began to question him. He didn't say a word. She struggled and fought her way to let go of his hand and once she succeeded she screamed "Who was that?"

"Please, let us just run."

"No, I want an explanation."

"Did you see her?"

"Yes she looked right at you."

"Lilith I don't know."

"What do you mean?"

"I mean maybe she is alive?"

"No that is just stupid!"

"Really, look at us, we are a creation for destruction."

"I just wanted some time with you."

"Lilith, I am sorry."

"Enzo, I am so upset."

"What did I do?"

"Not at you."

He held her hand "At least let me take you back."

Snatching her hand back "We will go there without holding hands."

His heart tore into two as if a knife had cut right through it and it started bleeding. He didn't show his face to Lilith the whole time they were together, because he knew if she saw his face, water would run down his eyes. He knew that both of them would not like it if she did look at him as he would physically smile but he inside he was emotionally drained and spiritually he felt dead. If even a tiny poke to have touched his delicate skin, he would have broken down and started crying. He hated all things that revolved around him and her.

They arrived back to the Benjamin suite and going up the elevator was the longest ride they have gone. Without saying a word a sense of dread was in the air. As they reached their floor, Lilith quickly walked past and Enzo followed up with her, leaving her at the door. His hat covered his eyes. She noticed that about Enzo, that he was a tough guy but his heart was soft if pierced right. Her hand touched his gentle face. Struggling to fight his feelings, his weakness was shown and a drop of water fell from his eyes. With this, his hat still covering his eyes, he saw the unthinkable at the edge of his hat, he saw droplets of tears pouring out of her eyes. Enzo looked her and she cried "Don't look at me."

His hand touched her face and he rubbed her tears "Stop crying, please."

"Why?"

"Because if you cry, I will definitely cry."

His lips touched her forehead, gently kissing it, leaving a stain for love and forgiveness. He went back to his room and fell into bed.

Hungry Eyes

In a college which looked like a castle, in which the architecture dated as far as 1700 to 1800. In the slightly pale yellow castle, the halls were spacious with grand staircases made out of shiny marble. The lights above were hung by straight wires. The interior of the building looked modern and yet old at the same time. The windows were quite modernized. The starry night twinkled bright with heavy rain coming down outside. Enzo wore a black heavy coat. In one hand a he had his black phone, messaging Emily, writing that he is in the college and coming there with her favourite cake, which was cheese cake with strawberry syrup on top with a little strawberry placed on top. He got two grilled cheese with ham and chicken and lastly, he got her favourite cappuccino, filled with a creamy topping and for himself, he got the same thing, as he knew that she would drink some of it and she would stealthy take his drink, but he didn't care. He would love it when he caught her and smiled with the straw in her mouth, looking at his eyes as he tilted her head down with her beautiful shiny hair covering her face. He would melt, if he saw her like that and she knew that he loved her so much every time he looked at her

The only thing she saw was his hungry eyes as he would always stare at her. She would usually turn around and check if there was something wrong with her, by using her hand mirror. Enzo would come from behind and rest her arms around her belly resting his head on her shoulder, gently kissing her neck as she would eventually turn around and look at his eyes, and in that brief moment of silence, both of them knew, even though they didn't say it, that both of them said in their minds that they loved each other. Being lost in a state of thought, he would usually day dream about her and that lovely smile.

Walking up the stairs, going towards the usually spacious hallway, he noticed something was wrong. He saw the place, filled with people outside, with their phones out recording something spontaneous, whispering words and rumours starting to spread. Enzo didn't usually care about those type of people or he didn't usually care about other people's problems except for himself or for Emily, he was already too love drunk. Walking towards the stairs, looking up to see if there was space for him to walk, but they all saw his face with sorrow in their faces, either looking down or away to avoid eye contact. Enzo ignored their expressions and continued going up in silence. The silence grew intense and people started to stare at him.

"What?" Enzo yelled, "Why are you looking at me?"

The crowd didn't say anything. Enzo was starting to get shivers up his spine and dreadful thoughts grew in his mind. What if Emily is involved in this? What if she is hurt? He would think much more dreadful thoughts but they were unaccepted from himself. He thought, possibly the worst thing that came to his mind was murder.

He walked slowly, getting there slower. Walking up the last bit of the stairs and seeing a glimpse of the destruction caused. Reached the point of no return, he saw the police pushing back the students behind the police crime investigation tape. He saw blood on the walls and a blade as though it had slashed through a body and the blood of the sword seemed to have landed on the wall. It was in a slanting streak of blood on the white wall of the dorm. He stopped walking, as time slowed down. He dropped everything with the coffee spilling on the floor and the cakes destroyed. He started to go a little closer, trying to shed some light into the matter, praying that nothing had happened to her. Pushing the crowd away from him, the police officer placed his hand on Enzo. Smacking it away, trying to get past the investigation tape as the police officers caught him and pushed back carrying him back as he screamed "Let me go!"

Enzo's eyes started to tear blood, pumping to his face as his anger and sadness grew. Resisting the officer pushing him back with all his force, furiously kicking and his arms flailing, trying to catch something to pull himself back.

Assigned to a new dorm room, it was the same blue room with a plant at the corner of the square room, a computer desk, dim light and a white light above him. Midnight with sitting up playing their favourite songs, as they were old souls.

Both of them were like old souls that loved old music. They would lie on the bed, listen to songs, lying down and talk about their day. Sometimes they wouldn't even say a word, but they said a million words by just lying down and looking at their eyes. He would like it when she would hug him when he came back from college and both of them would cheer each other up by either Emily playing the very simple trick by easily kissing him when he wasn't expecting it or when she was angry he would just go out and bring back her favourite cheese cake. Crying by the very fact that he would think of the very fragment of the memory, would bring water to his eyes, grabbing the pillow, squeezing it tight, covering his face with the bed all messed up. Upset by the fact that he blamed himself for leaving her alone. Moreover, he was upset by the fact that he couldn't remember what they were even fighting over. The only thing he remembered was that what he did was unreasonable and he could have been sophisticated and taken another approach. He decided to bring her flowers but he knew that she wasn't a flower type of girl, so he bought her favourites, to make sure that she would be able to forgive him. He was quite happy when he bought it, excited to give them to her. But that day will never come, the day where he never ever be able to say sorry to the girl that he loved so much. The ring he'd bought for her was never going to land on her finger.

He woke up from a dream, sweating around his cheeks and forehead. He got up, removing his shirt, increasing the air conditioning and threw his sheets aside. He wasn't used to sleeping alone. He grabbed the cold pillow, tightening it between his chest, resting his head on the pillow and falling asleep, he wanted human contact once again.

Don't let me Drown

In the base of operations, the whole team was there drinking coffee and listening to music. Enzo came to the board room and saw all of them. He fell flat on the chair without any emotions in him as if he was a zombie. They were discussing how to pull out the leader to reveal himself when his operations has been foiled. Hans focused on his little brother. Over the weeks Logan and Hans' relationship with Dante, Enzo and Lilith had increased a lot and he considered them brothers, as a family, thus making Enzo the little brother.

Hans said "Didn't get any sleep?"

Suddenly someone said "Of course he didn't, he saw me."

Dante suddenly turned, knocking his chair and pulling out a pistol and aimed it straight at Emily, the woman in the white robes. Logan and Hans followed up with Hans pulling out his crossbow with Jonathan with his hands to the side and bowing down at the spiritual image.

"Emily?"

"Hello Dante."

"Who is she?"

"What so she isn't a ghost?

"She is or was Enzo's dead girlfriend? And she isn't a ghost."

"I am an angel."

"We are so screwed if God sent an angel."

"What do you want?" Enzo got up from his lifeless body and turned to her.

"Enzo could you explain why you are not shocked?"

"I saw her before."

"To answer Enzo, to tell you your next course of plan."

"What you are helping us?"

"Well there is the Judgement day."

"Why are angels involved in this."

"If you have forgotten, that now the ancient humans are free of choice."

"And?"

"They decided to join the army of darkness."

"That's why they are more or less likely to be demons?"

"Yes, so I volunteered to help this particular group."

"Wait so you mean that in the Judgement day there are four factions fighting?"

"Yes, the ancient humans, angels, demons and then there is you."

"So God is looking at us?"

"Yes, so I came to watch over Enzo and this bitch."

"Never call her that. I thought you were an angel of God." Enzo furiously shouted.

"No."

"I knew it was you who was watching us on our date."

"What, you guys had a date?"

"Well I wanted to say hi."

"By scaring me?"

"Maybe."

"Alright everyone shut up!" Logan shouted.

"Yeah agreeing with Logan, we got an angel on our side."

"So how much damage can an angel do?"

"Angels are not like the ancient humans that are made for war, but angels are made for healing and destruction if necessary, but since I've become an angel I've learnt how to fight all the factions."

"So you're a different angel?"

"I am a guardian angel, the highest ranks."

"Wait, I don't get it, the body was missing?" explained by Lilith.

"I was already an angel, I was watching over Enzo and Dante, but I became attached to him and as we fought, he left and the ancient human came by, to make it look like a murder, but his poor timing killed him and I had to leave, as I would have been questioned."

A hole in Enzo's soul was being repaired, being away from her but realising that she'd used him to get closer to him, as it was her mission, the hole was getting deeper and deeper. It was drowning him more and more.

They all knew that they got an angel as an ally but Enzo wasn't so sure about her being an ally, he was more concerned about Lilith. How could he protect her if the angel had someone who identifies her as an enemy rather than a friend?

"I do not want Emily close to her."

"Don't you trust me?"

"Is that even a question?"

"So what do you propose?"

"Lilith stays with me."

"Sounds good."

Emily's eyes shunned both of them. She wanted to get Enzo back on her side but, blinded by love he couldn't move on with Emily.

"So what abilities do you have?"

She summoned out a sword with divine inscription on it, by a flash of light "Its kills anyone by this blade."

"It looks like a normal sword but the inscriptions on it, what does it say?"

"Hell have no fury like I do."

"Could you engrave this on our swords?" stylishly said by Enzo.

"It will take time but it is possible, but I won't engrave Lilith's blade."

"Alright!" swiftly said by Dante.

"No Dante!"

"Enzo think about it, we are getting weapons in which a small cut can kill them."

"We are not negotiating with an angel, it's a devil in disguise."

"Do you think of me like that?"

"Yes!"

"Enzo, we do not want to start fights but you are right to get angry." Dante shouted.

"I know she wants Lilith dead for a fact."

"How about we try to trust her?"

"Fine."

Enzo took out his blade and tossed it on the table where they placed their coffee. The rest of the team placed their weapons on the table. He looked at Lilith and approached her, he pulled her sword, tossing it to the table. Jonathan passed his sword gently. She looked at Logan "Any weapons?"

"No I do not use!"

"Now engrave it and I could start trusting. Take Lilith's room and she will stay with me."

"How do you know she knows Lilith's room?"

"She watched us all the way."

He stormed out without saying another word. Knowing that they got a couple of weeks, until the day of the apocalypse. Up in his room lying on his bed, thinking about the worst that could happen. He mostly thought of Lilith dying or his brother dying, he couldn't handle the thought of what could happen. He just wanted this day to end. He went back to his room and decided to sleep due to the jet lag he had.

Suddenly a red alert was wailing and Enzo pushed himself off his bed and went outside. Rushing towards the elevator and heading down, as the elevator opened a large group of Benjamin's private army, created a wall of people standing side by side with weapons in their hands. They were wearing swat uniforms but instead of Swat it said Security. It formed a little further from the entrance, protecting the hallways and reception desk. Enzo hurried out of the elevator and saw a man in a suit with black long hair tied up and has a massive black beard with brown eyes with his hands up "I would like to speak to Enzo or Dante."

"Well hello there." Looking at Enzo.

"Who are you?" Enzo quick drew his pistol, behind the swat forces.

"Please do not shoot, I am just a simple messenger."

"What is your name and what do you want messenger?"

Hans looked at the camera feeds and saw Enzo alone with the swat squad with an ancient human. Dante quickly ran towards his little brother. The rest of the group found their way to Enzo regrouping with him.

"The full group is here. My name is Drakkar."

"Okay what do you want?" Logan shouted.

"I just wanted to say that Judgement Day is close at hand."

"So why are you warning us when we know about it?"

"We always are polite to warn our enemies to surrender or die."

"Death doesn't sound so bad."

"It is your funeral, you are like the rest who tried to save this world, just destined to die."

Noticing the angel on their side.

"I didn't know angels supported ancient humans?"

"We only support the ones who are on earth's side and have guts."

"We will see on the battlefield, arch angel Emily."

He turned around with one foot and walked off casually mocking them. They knew that it was going to be one hell of a day.

I need aid

Enzo was in his hotel suite in the Benjamin building. He started to flick through his phone, going through the job selection of many jobs, in which the new industries got in and wanted to remove their competition but they decided to do it the dirty way. The more experienced you are, the more money you get. Enzo really liked a job that was suited for him and Lilith, since Jonathan and Dante are a duo and so are Logan and Hans. Suddenly, he got a call from Lilith. Enzo thought it was coincidence that she'd tried to reach him, when he was about to call her.

"Hey," Enzo said "I was about to call you."

"Hey Enzo," Lilith choked "help me."

"Where are you?" Enzo was assertive as he heard her tone. A tone he never wanted to hear from her.

The phone was taken away from her and the anonymous person told him that he needed one million in cash. The call was dropped, his outrage brewed as he would not give them the money but he wanted to give them a swift end as they touched the one thing that he swore to himself, he would shelter. He sprinted towards Benjamin, knocking on his door, harshly opening it without Benjamin saying 'come in' or if he had a meeting. Fortunately he wasn't busy "Yes Enzo," Benjamin politely said "what's the matter?"

"Benjamin, someone's got Lilith." Enzo said panting "I am going."

"Wait, let me call the team to give you back up."

"No time." He rushed out without giving Benjamin a chance to call the team.

He went into one of the fastest cars he could possibly rally from the Benjamin district. Getting in it, he found a text message from Lilith. "Chop, chop," it said "time is ticking." It gave the location to a specific harbour that Enzo knew. It could be a warehouse that either both of them would die in or survive, but he was ready to take the risk. He didn't want to make a second mistake and leave Lilith all by herself waiting for him. Dodging moving vehicles and red lights, he needed to get there, no matter what. He wanted her alive. He needed her alive.

He stopped in from off the harbour with his foot pushing down the brake's black imprints behind, as it skidded, trying to stop as the vehicle body kit moved slightly forward. As it came to a complete stop, the body kit went back to normal. He got out of his car as he didn't buckle in his seatbelt, he didn't want to waste a second. He went to the trunk and got out the briefcase. He grabbed it with one hand, took a deep breath and opened the large doors. It looked like an aircraft hangar. He saw Lilith with her hair covering her face, looking down, lifeless as if she had no soul. He slowly walked with loud steps of his shoes, as he walked through the massive room towards her. Reaching her, he placed the briefcase near her wooden chair, placed his warm hands on her very icy bitter face, seeing a fragment of her pale face, he gulped down the fear in his eyes. Getting ready, sticking his tongue out and squeezing his lips to his tongue, praying that it wasn't what he thought it was. He slightly pressed her head pushing it up, he whispered "Oh my god." As her face was worn out struggling to breath. The lights came on, looking at a single person, came out with a few of the guys behind him "Well she is doing fine for now."

 Enzo got up clenching his fits with his muscles flexing and his veins popping as he looked at him "Who did it?"

 He said "My henchmen behind you."

 Enzo turned around and saw a couple of henchmen, he started to punch them as they retaliated hitting him with steel pipes. They were mere mercenaries, in which they didn't think that Enzo could possibly be an ancient human. Enzo recklessly taking hits as the more he was being hit at, the more it made him berserk.

Deflecting the steel pipe by grabbing it, pulling it and extending his arm, jabbing his nose letting go of the pipe. He broke the pipe in half, instead of him having the advantage, he wanted to crack their morale before he kills them. He looked behind him and saw the leader trying to take him down but Enzo pulled out a knife from his coat, ducking down, stabbing his hip, removing it and grabbing his arm and stabbed him under the armpit, right between the bones to stop his movement. As a result, he kicked him down, making him suffer on the hard grey surface as he wanted to kill the ones who hurt Lilith. He slowly walked towards them, reaching behind his hip, as he pulled out another dagger, reverse gripping it as he ran towards a bunch of them instantly stabbing them in the neck as he was going on an executioner streak with rapid combos with the daggers by stabbing the chest, reaching inside his pocket pulling out really small sharpened dagger like needles, tossed at the opposite enemy without looking, as he used the dagger to finish off the victim, he started by a clean kill under the chin piercing upwards. They would like to tip the odds by pulling out their knives and counter attacking their attacks, he would strike their mouths opening a significance amount of flesh with blood spilling everywhere or he would dodge slitting their eyes or their throat to finish them off. Unlike his brother, Enzo liked to stylishly kill his enemies, while Dante was more like the serious type, he would be able to kill and he would take his chances. Blood painted on his black clothes, he removed a cloth and wiped his blade, pushing the cloth back in his coat as he finished hacking and slashing beautifully at his new found enemies. He turned around and saw the leader's face scared out of shock. "How!" Enzo's eyes looked dead towards the world, he saw Lilith as he cut open the ropes. Her body flew to him as he was kneeling down, her head went over his shoulder her arms straight with limited blood flowing through her veins as the ropes were so tight. He rubbed her back to comfort her. He looked across the distance. He pulled out his gun and shot him three times.

"Don't worry," he whispered to Lilith "I got you."

He lifted her off the ground as he went, turning around sharply. He went towards the car, pushing her over his shoulder as her lifeless body was dangling a bit. He put her in the car, gently strapping on her seat belt and pushing her hair back behind her ears, she never seemed to like her ears but Enzo always thought and said very lovely things about her to boost her confidence. He went to check her, he grabbed her hand to check her pulse and touched her neck to find out if there was a pulse. He wanted to make sure he wasn't too late. He went back and grabbed the suitcase.

"I knew it was a trap." The leader said choking.
"No." Enzo replied "I would had given the money."
"What!"
"For Lilith I would had given you the million."
"How did you know?"
"About the ambush?" Enzo said "There is a price on every hitman's head." After a hitman would carry out the missions successfully, they would want to have a hit on their head but clearing out that bounty would be quite hard as they would have to lay low and make sure that no one should hire them.

"I thought I would roll the dice." laughing as he choked on his own blood.

"Do you want me to end you?" Enzo had compassion to end the dear man, as he didn't want to see him choking on his own blood, dying in a horrible way.

"Please and thank you."

Enzo pulled out his gun, kneeling down pointing at his head and shot him three more times. He took a deep breath sheathing his weapon back made the sigh of the cross and left back to check up on Lilith. He saw Lilith, resting peacefully. He went in the car and drove carefully as he didn't want to wake her up.

In the Benjamin building, he brought her back to her place, checking her face as her scars and wounds seemed to have healed, he kissed her forehead and tucked her into bed. He saw Benjamin telling him about the fantastic news that she was alive. He thanked Benjamin for lending the money in case it was an emergency that he couldn't handle. But what Enzo really feared was, what if it was Shade or if it was one of the leaders of the war. Giving back the money, as Benjamin declined it and told him to keep it as is it his reward, Benjamin called back up as he took care of the job. Enzo knew that his reward was not seeing Lilith die. He didn't want to make the same mistake twice.

Emily was disappointed as she saw the whole thing. She was a bit upset that Enzo would go so far for that girl. Emily already sensed her powers and knew that she was quite strong but her powers will not evoke that easily. Enzo went to see Lilith, to see if she was alright. Opening the door, he saw her about to open the door.
"Hey!" she said.
"Hey" he replied.
"Thanks for saving me."
"Next time." he said "Don't leave without me."
"What do you mean?"
"I mean you have a duo partner." he said "Never go without me."
He extended his hand and said "Come on."
"Where?"
"I want to take you for an ice cream."
"Really?"
"Yeah."
"Why?" as she held his hand.
"Well, I want to make you happy."

Hope

Two days until Judgement day and everyone was called into the board room by Enzo. Leaning back on the board, waiting peacefully with everyone in the room besides Logan. Emily was staring at Lilith as she was trying to ignore her as she didn't want to cause any fights or arguments between them. Dante's hands were crossed and his feet were on the table, shaking them to kill his boredom. Hans popped his cigarette from his pack placed it on his mouth, opened the window and started smoking. Jonathan was sitting down with his new found clothes, in which he wore casual clothes, admiring his red and black square patterned shirt. Suddenly, Logan opened the door and he looked totally different, he'd shaved his hair and left a strip in the middle. He'd gelled his mohawk to spike it up but not fully up as he didn't want to look like an obnoxious person, like a douche-bag. Everyone looked at him with awe. Logan hated getting stared at "What?"

"Looking good."

"Yeah!"

"I wish at the monastery, I had a haircut."

"Thanks, I would like to look pretty when I die in the next three days."

"Alright, I called you all here because Lilith and I talked about the plan."

"Alright so tell us the plan."

"The four of you guys will fight against the hundreds of them."

"Wait you mean me, Hans, Jonathan and Emily will only fight them alone. That's a shit plan" Logan screamed.

"Yeah if you were alone."

"What?"

"Lilith will support you from a sniper's point, on top of the building along with two other snipers from Benjamin's private army."

"What about you and me, Enzo?"

"We are going to find the leader and take him down."

"I don't get this plan." Emily got up screaming.

"A leader does not fight, he watches his mistakes and makes use of them in the next fight."

"I don't get this, we are going into a mindless slaughter."

"Emily you are an angel. You heal and protect."

"Archangel."

"So what is the difference?" Hans explained.

"There are only 100 archangels in existence, counting me. Archangels are as powerful as all the angels, they are also more combat wise than angels."

"What can they do?"

"They have permission to kill and have additional powers from angels besides healing."

"What powers?"

"Like the sword engraving with special runes to kill darkness, speaking with the dead, summoning the dead and lastly, resurrection."

"Wait resurrection?"

"I can resurrect someone but at a price."

"What price?"

"Someone on earth dies in his place."

"No one is going to die." shouted Enzo.

"Alright so how do we find the leader?"

"We will go to the tower next to the Benjamin's building."

"Why there?"

"To check out the building on top, to have a good viewpoint of the battlefield."

"Why this is pointless!"

"No, this is like playing chess, we knew he would strike this building because we took out all of his expansions for money, his only place is to take this building for money."

"So you know their plan?" Emily questioned swiftly.

"Yeah it's to make humans do their dirty work."

"Wait, do you know why?"

"Not really?"

"They are lost souls like you, but the leader is not part of the army of darkness, he is trying to find a place in the afterlife to make a deal with the Reaper to destroy heaven."

"So he is not only destroying his creation but his kingdom in heaven by getting himself to purgatory and opening the gates to the afterlife to send his army to kill the one man who saved the earth?"

"You mean God?"

"No, your father!"

"Goddammit!"

The conversation got really serious as they knew that the only protectors of earth rest on their shoulders.

"So Logan, tank, Hans shall help him. Lilith will shoot them and Emily, you can support Logan and Hans. That's the plan."

"I said it once and I will say it again. That plan is shit but I will go with it."

The Three worlds

The sky wasn't right. The sky looked odd, it was pitch black with the clouds covering the starry night, only the moon shining brightly. 11:00 in the morning, Judgement day was just an hour away. Lilith woke up lying in bed, unable to sleep, unable to or to feel she was in an absolute state of nothingness. She lay in bed looking at the ceiling and thinking about how she would cope if Enzo were to just fall down one day and die. She didn't want that day to be today. She went and put on her protective armour and it slipped over her arms, legs and chest, strapping it in to secure and tighten it. She looked at a massive silver sniper rifle with a scope and a long barrel. With a small note attached to it.

Sorry Lilith,
I wanted to give your weapon downstairs
but time was ticking and I wouldn't have been able
to meet you and I didn't want to disturb you.
Ps. could you wear red lipstick today, I think you
will look good in it as I saw it outside on the table.

Love Enzo

Picking up the sniper, grabbing its ammo, penetrated it and cocks the bullet. She looked at herself in the mirror and started combing her hair, she saw the red lipstick on the dressing table. She took it out and applied it firmly on her lips, pressing it down on her very smoothly. Holding her rifle with both of her hands as she got out of the room and went to the elevator, reaching the bottom floor, completely empty with no businessmen. Usually there would be people around, even the receptionist was gone. She went down to the base of operations and she saw Hans and Logan with Emily. Dante came into the room, following behind her.

"I hate you." she noticed the red lipstick.

"Stop it!" Enzo walked into the room.

"Huh, you told her."

"Emily, I will tell you this once. Touch her and you will face me."

A guard ran into the commotion and said "Sir we got a problem."

"What is it?"

"They are outside."

Fright in their eyes as they stared towards Enzo "Party time."

Walking towards the glass entrance of the Benjamin building, outside there were thousands of them standing bloodthirsty, vicious lost souls as if they were a pack of wolves stalking its prey.

Logan muttered "I like the odds of four against a thousand."

"The way of the wanderer is the lonely yet deadly."

"Lilith got up with the other snipers. Emily, Logan and Hans stay here."

Logan saw the messenger in front of the army wearing his suit and tie smartly, unlike the rest.

Logan shouted "What are you doing here?"

"I am Drakkar the messenger and general of this army."

"You lying piece of shit, I knew I should have killed you when I had the chance."

"Yes I knew you would because if you'd known who I was, you would have.

It was about fifteen minutes until it hits Judgement day. Logan was scratching his head and starting to cross his hands, slightly tapping his right foot and leaning towards the left, waiting to kill him as he hates people who lie or deceive him. Emily, at the side of Logan, summoning her sword by extending her hand and then clutching the handle, as the weapon slowly forged into a katana. Next to Emily, with his crossbow in his hand, with a fine line separating them and the walkers. Hans said "I thought you liked a western long sword."

"I like katanas better now."

Thunder in the air as she looked up "Rain."

Rain pouring down on their heads. Staring down the two armies, looking at each other with blood lust in their eyes. Flowing down Logan's beard, his blue eyes staring down, piercing their black souls, he wore a black modified suit that made him look like a tank without sleeves showing his muscles. Jonathan with his Shaolin monk robes instead of his monastery robes standing stiff with his eyes showing that same blood lust. Logan clashed his hands together with his left hand as a fist and the right as his palm. His outfit was like that of a shaolin warrior with a yellow cloth shirt, yellow trousers with the white cloth covering his legs up till his knee with robes binding it. Lastly, he wore black slip on shoes, this made him flexible. He could kick and punch much more efficiently, making him much faster, with his mind able to strike fast he would be able to find the weak points and strike it. He slowly bowed down with his face looking at the thousands of foes. "Blood will be shed on this day."

Lilith went to the highest point in the Benjamin's building. She saw three snipers up there reloading their weapons, putting bullets in their clips and checking their weapons. Walking through "Get ready guys we got ten minutes."

She walked to the window and laid her clips at her lap, placing on her lap waiting patiently looking through her scope, watching Emily and the army of darkness rising. Getting an uneasy feeling whenever she sees her.

Thunder cracked, the rain poured. Suddenly, Drakkar roared, running with all the walkers behind him heading towards Logan. Hans got behind them and started shooting in the battlefield. Pulling the cigarette from his coat, putting it in in his mouth and threw the rest of the packet on the concrete floor, lighting it with his zip lighter with the words 'Lady Killer' engraved on it. He immediately put it back in and started shooting with his crossbow. Logan ran in like the psychopath he was, without any hesitation of death clashing with the army. Lilith was on the roof top shooting her sniper rifle, with each shot, her hair flew due to the recoil being too powerful getting pushed back a little bit. Emily was running through them by inflicting as little as a paper cut to kill them as she jumped, rolled or even encountered them to manage to kill them. Logan was running towards the walkers with furious rage by punching their heads, they were immediately dead otherwise Hans would finished them off with a clean shot to the head. If they focused, Hans supporting Logan he would inhale his smoke and go behind them and shoot them or he would knock them back and lastly point the mini crossbow on their head and finish them off. Jonathan walking, as one by one, they came close to him, he would punch so fast that the rain water from the bodies that he punched, flew out as he kept punching and kicking. If they tried to attack from the back, attempting to catch him off guard, they would meet a swift end by a knuckle punch from the back, without even looking, by raising his arm behind him, the freshly tapped bandages on his fists were soon blood soaked and slightly washed away from the rain. Extending his arm back, shooting the mini crossbow at the walker, sneaking up on them, Logan massacred all the walkers near him as the general saw him. Logan looked at his wet suit, removing his coat, staring at his blood soaked body, his death staring eyes and tightening his fists. Logan grabbed and ripped the jaw of the walker with ease "Come on Drakkar, Lets Fight." Both of them slowly walked towards each other, slowly increasing their speed thus ran towards each other. Screaming at each other "You smell good." The minions paved the way for their battle. Logan jumped, getting Drakkar on the floor, pinned down, kneeling down and repeatedly punching as his face tried to get up but his head was bouncing on the floor cracking up his skull and opening a wound. Struggling to get up, Drakkar managed to kick him back. Logan was trying to get up when Drakkar got him in a lock position and gently pushed him to the floor. Grabbing him from the back and smashing his face, breaking his nose, cutting his lip and damaging his cheek bones. Fading away from reality he said, "Do you like death?" His eyes slowly closing as a small blood pool emerged from blood and rain water around his face. Into a state of memory, he saw him being alone in the orphanage and no one wanting to play with him. He was either too big to be a child or he was found to be scary in nature, he made children cry by just looking at him. Shunned by society and left by his unknown parents, he was about to commit suicide until a boy came up to him "Hi." he remembered Hans. He saw Dante and him playing drinking games and he got drunk. He remembered that smart comeback Enzo gave him when he used to insult his stupid mistakes and his weird love life. He couldn't stand the fact of him dying to know he had found his family. He didn't want to die!

Logan's eyes opened as Drakkar left him to die as he went to get his coat. He noticed something weird and saw Logan's big eyes cursing him from afar.

Blood trickling down his head, rain hitting his face he is a man with little words but his actions speak much louder. His fists steadily glowed blood red and it looked as if it was on fire with the aura surrounding it and a flame like tattoo scarring his skin. Logan looking down "I am angry" he said in the calmest way. Dropping his coat, "I should had finished you but I do not make the same mistakes twice." He walked up to Logan with his blood soaked face as the rain was cleaning the blood and his wounds. He looked at his eyes and tried to jab Logan. Dodging it, his fist moved like the speed of light and smashed his face. Flipping him over as he landed in the sloppy back flip hitting the concrete floor as his head bounced on the floor before reaching a total state of death. It looked like a blood bath around him, he fell down on his knees as his flaming glowing fist started to fade away and the scaring started to heal. Logan's pain resistance as he trained himself by using stapling his full arm and then pulling it out to discipline himself to ignore pain. Screaming for the first time in pain near death that even a tiny scratch would have taken this beast down. A walker coming behind hearing the steps of the walker coming closer and closer, hearing each step, his fate was sealed ready to die as he was ready since the time he was young. No regrets and no repentance, all he wanted was to rest in peace. Suddenly, a bolt was shot at a walker, as a smoke like figure went behind Logan "Like I'd let you die."

"Huh looks like you saved me again."

Emily walked right through the walkers without breaking a sweat or energy "Oh you guys tired?"

"Yeah just a flesh wound."

She placed her one hand on Logan's head as a yellow light sparkling through her hand. Regaining his energy and healing his wounds much faster, but the walkers became more violent without a leader. They went on a total rampage, biting each other and killing one another focusing on Logan, Hans and Emily looking at them as they said "You smell good."

With little remaining, they quickly executed them without hassle. They saw Jonathan in the distance leaving a body count behind him. "Awh shik that guy is getting ahead of me!" Logan shouted "I won't let him win the body count."

"Well Enzo was right, three against a thousand was a fun idea."

Jonathan started getting tired. He fell to the ground, his knee and his fist touching the ground and the other placed at his chest gasping for breath. He got up, looked straight, rolling up his sleeves with twenty kilograms of weight strapped to both of his arms and legs. He unstrapped both of them, grabbing it with both of his arms and throwing it on the ground with it cracking the ground slightly. He twisted his neck left and right, got into a shaolin position, a walker brave enough to face him ran towards him in that same position, as the walker slowed and fell flat on the ground. The walker had a massive hole near its chest, blood pouring out as the rain continued. He was so fast that he was to remain in the same position. He walked slowly as walkers dropped dead on the floor. He then got the walker's attention, as he pulled out a flask and started drinking it. Logan said "Holy shit."

"What's that?"

"The most dangerous bottle in the world."

"What's in it?"

"Ten mixtures of alcohol." Logan said "The most dangerous technique drunken fist."

Jonathan drank the full bottle of alcohol. His vision became blurry, as he started swaying side to side, moving his hands up and down like a slithering like a snake. A walker looked as if he was stunned as a result, he tried to attack Jonathan but met a tragic end.

Enzo and Dante went to the opposite building and went to the top floor. They went up in the elevator. In the elevator, Enzo started humming.

Dante looking straight ahead started humming as well.

The elevator dinged and the both of them came out, slightly in shock. They saw a black figure looking out the window in the dark room with very few lights lit and he stood in the dark looking at his failure of an army.

"Well, what do we have here?"

"Hello blood brothers." He turned around with his face blacked out.

"We are here to end it."

"Do you know who taught the Spartans?"

"Great history lessons."

"We taught the Spartans how to fight, we started world war one and two, trying to destroy the world but Hitler listened to us nicely, until he grew selfish and didn't listen to us and he lost."

"So you are the ones destroying the world peace?"

"That's the Apocalypse plan, not to destroy the world but the humans shall do it and the humans will kill themselves, the humans will cause chaos as they are racists who do not care about anyone else."

"Enough history lessons." Dante pulled out his sword with the runes glowing.

"Wait, Dante something is wrong."

"What is it?"

"Who are you?"

"I am the leader."

"I didn't know he would come here." Enzo whispered.

"Wait, so we are basically screwed."

"Yeah."

Sprinting back as the elevator closed in the nick of time as their hands smacked the elevators doors.

"What do we do now?"

"I don't know I think we are screwed."

"Shit."

They turned around and got out their swords. He walked a little closer looking at their faces, they saw a young man with perfectly good hair and a neatly shaven beard covering is face. No weapons and wearing a black robe with a rope around his waist. Neatly tied with the two ropes hanging in front of each other. There are engravings on the sleeves of the robes like designs of honour for a battle veteran.

"How are you young?"

"Perks of being ancient human."

"You know what they say, heroes live long enough to become villains."

"But I am different from those outside your company of three fought."

"Let us see!"

He drew closer, throwing the first strike with his blade. Enzo with the second strike simultaneously charging in like bulls with no aim. He parried or evaded every slash and kick in which a combination was given. Intense sparing as Dante reached to a conclusion to kick him out of frustration. Pushing him back "Big mistake."

Dusting his robe, he looked at Enzo paying full attention to him as he tried to finish him off but he disarmed Enzo, took his daggers in a hostage position and threw them at Dante recklessly. Recklessly dodging as it missed by his skin, opening a cut. Enzo broke free and tried to punch him. Countered by Enzo, shaped his hand in a palm stroked his throat and punched his face with blood gushing out of his nose and mouth knocked down, lastly stomping on his arm as he heard the sound of a bone breaking. He grabbed Dante's sword with his bare hands sliding it, blood gushing out of it, punched him in his stomach, broke his arm and kicked him down. Throwing his blade away, both of them on the floor, giving up he said "This reminds me of another situation."

"What?"

"Yes Enzo I will take away Lilith, you will know how it feels like to finally lose someone."

"Don't listen to him Enzo!"

Not admitting defeat, Enzo and Dante tried to find another situation where they could fight. No options were given. On the verge of frustration and anger as the leader was skipping and whistling along, twisting his head left and right walking away from them, limping towards him"I will kill you!"

"Try."

Dante and Enzo screamed in pain as Dante held his left eye and Enzo held his right eye. The leader looked in surprise as he turned back thinking they had gone insane. Their eyes were glowing as the glimpse of light pasted their hands, bright red light. They got shaking a bit, Dante grabbed his hand and twisted it back. Their eyes closed as they got up. Opening it, their eyes were blood moon red touching the pupil, slowly fading in color towards orange until it reaches the edge of the iris in which it has a very dark shade of orange in Dante's left and Enzo's right. Dante got up, fixing his arm. Enzo got up and clutched his loose arm. A thunder like sound as Enzo fixed it by pushing it up.

"Oh you are not humans."

"Leave her alone, you are not done with me."

Looking at both of them "Wow the blood brothers show their passion."

He walked towards them "I will not make the same mistake, by not killing you."

Dante and Enzo fought with great succession of punches, jabs and kicks. If he were to counter them, their eyes would know where he would attack, thus slowing down the time when he attacks, they could dodge or counter as their eyes could now manipulate time and slow it down. Dante pulled out his dagger and as soon as he countered Dante, he held his hand and stabbed his arm and piercing his neck with the dagger, he pulled it out from his coat. Blood pouring out. He then smashed his face by a divesting punch. Pushing him down to the floor, eyes dead locked and there was no return. Sweating with blood on their faces, Enzo went to get his sword as was Dante. Suddenly, Dante got kicked by the leader from the back. He grabbed his sword, rushing towards Enzo, stabbing him in the stomach. His eyes dilating and his red eye started to move around violently. Looking at the situation, he reacted by scrabbling to find his sword. Grabbing it, he pierced it through his heart spitting out blood all over. "I will not die!"

He removed the blade and stabbed Enzo again repeatedly, thus he stopped as he was out of breath. Pulling out his gun in his side, putting it under his chin and shot him. Raining Blood for a second as Enzo fell down out of lack of energy, as if he had no life support. Dante picked up his lifeless body and took him to the elevator, lying down on his brothers thighs, trying to opening his eyes, but the excruciating pain was inflicting him and his wounds were not getting better. He knew it was grievous wounds. Trying to open his eyes he saw his brothers looking down at him. Tears in his eyes "Not you Enzo, first Quinton, not you as well." He whispered "I couldn't protect you. I killed Quinton."

"Why God!" He yelled.

He took him outside in the rain, Enzo trying to open his eyes saw Lilith, he didn't know if she was crying or not.

Dante took him inside and put him in the clinic bed, blood spewing out of his chest into Dante's hands as he looked at it. Stitching him up and applying bandage struggling to survive as Dante looking as his dying corpse, he saw Quinton and remembered that he was useless but he wasn't going to let that happen as he had a plan. Fell to unconscious. Dante looked at his struggling face.

Dante cried "Emily heal my brother!"

"No!"

Drawing out his blade with his glowing red eye sticking it at her throat "No?" he said "Heal my brother!"

"He is almost dead!"

"Almost!"

"I want him in purgatory and he will be with me forever."

Touching her throat "I will destroy the world if I do not have him."

His eye glowing darker and darker towards the shade of black.

She went to the side cautiously and stuck her hand on his head releasing a yellow light on Enzo. Coughing bad blood, he was breathing normally taking deep breaths.

Walking away as the blade was still at her throat "Leave Emily."

She turned her back and walked away from the clinic. "He was going to survive with or without my healing."

"How!"

"He cannot be killed like the walkers, you and your gang are immortals but not Gods there are ways to kill you but even if a tiny fragment of your life is there, you will regenerate."

"Leave now!"

"Goodbye Enzo." She whispered in his ear and kissed his cheek.

"Nice meeting you Dante."

She walked out of the building and vanished.

Tea time

Enzo with the salty smell in his nose, lying down on something soft yet jagged, he moved his hands slowly swaying left to right, rubbing this soft yet distorted bed, it was slightly wet but it was not cold or hot but the right temperature. The salty water gushed to his face as he opened his eyes, getting up looking at the slightly grey sky with a hint of sunlight. Getting up, he saw the beach with the waves meeting the shore. It was very clean and vast. The sea looked like it could go on forever without any sight of land. Enzo wondered if someone had teleported him towards a deserted island.

"The beach? I was just with Dante?" he whispered "Where am I?" He turned left and saw nothing but rocks and stones in the sand. He turned right and saw something odd and out of place. He saw a table with three chairs and contents on the table. "Well maybe I am just crazy," he said "or I'm just seeing this."

Enzo would generally speak alone to give himself a confidence boost, because without his brother he felt insecure whether he was making the right choice or not.

It looked quite far, but he was ready to make a move towards them. The more he walked, he saw something is the distance, he cannot decide what is it. Walking a bit further, confused trying to recall events that have happened before reaching here and thinking about what is that object he is walking towards. The table wasn't that big and was shaped as a square with two very royally made chairs opposite of each other. The table was filled with chocolate chip cookies, freshly baked, steaming without any burnt ends. Biscuits with chocolate fillings in between the biscuits. There were cake pieces in which it was sliced perfectly, with a slightly dark honey colour on the cake. The scones, which looked slightly sweetened and one glazed with jam and honey dips in one plate. Sandwiches placed very neatly and presented in a form of a pyramid with each side having a different contents. In one, it had grilled ham, beef and cheese. In the other one, it had jam and cream cheese, lastly, the last one had salmon with chives and cheese. In the very middle of the table was a tea pot in which the smell made his mouth water due to the aromas of the food and the slightly gingered tea.

He looked at the wooden seats and saw a piece of paper in a rectangle shape, to keep it standing with a name written on it left on the table. He picked up one of the reservations lists and saw the name written in beautiful cursive, which frightened him. His eyes dilated with a drop of sweat coming out from his temple, his hand shaking rapidly and gently placing it back to its original position. It said 'the devil'. He went around to the other chair, opposite to his and picked it up. He was shocked to see who he would have a cup of tea with was god. Enzo was confused and had many questions on his mind. But the questions that struck him the most were written on the third chair. He looked around him and saw no one in sight, only himself. He picked it up slowly with his hand extending out of his way, grabbing the paper and taking a good long look to what he had read. Surprised and unaware to what he had read that it was his name.

"Sit down son" someone said. Enzo looked at the Devil's seat and saw a well-groomed man with his semi long hair slicked down wearing a black suit. "Please sit," he said "God will arrive soon."

Enzo carefully sat down. "Don't worry my good boy," he gently said "I will never harm you."

"You are the devil!"

"Yes, yes I am."

This send shivers down Enzo's spine, being uneasy with the man who caused so much destruction and chaos in the world that it was unbearable to fight him, as he knew that he wouldn't last a fight not even a second against the prince of darkness.

"What do you want?" Enzo roared slightly.

"A scone please."

"Okay" God said.

Enzo looked to his left and saw a person glowing slightly white and he was unable to see his face.

"Wait Devil," he said "guests first?"

"Oh yes, I completely forgot my manners."

"Thank you." Enzo stuttered out of confusion. Enzo bit the scone as he screamed "Delicious!"

"Yes it is. I prepared it." the devil said.

Enzo spat it out "Were you going to poison me?" God laughed so much and the devil's face went numb as he was hurt "Why does every human hate me?"

"Well maybe you were always the bad guy from the start."

"Times change, God."

"So Where am I?"

"You are in purgatory."

"What!"

"You are dead."

"Awh man."

"Wait a minute."

"Oh myself." God said "Dev that's Xander's son."

"Oh yeah," he said "look at him."

"Guys please." Enzo cried "Why am I here."

Enzo's tears started coming out, but he wasn't crying. "Why am I crying?"

"Well Enzo you are dead!" The devil said while eating one of the sandwiches.

"And you are crying," God replied "because in purgatory you cannot hide your feelings."

"What do you mean?"

"Well you are desperate to go back home."

"Of course he is!" the devil said "He wants to see his brother."

"Any sandwiches?"

God grabbed the sandwiches and started eating with the wind blowing in the air.

"Delicious." God said.

"Thank you." The devil graciously replied.

"So how are you guys in a good relationship?" Enzo questioned.

"What do you mean?" the devil said.

"Well you are having tea." he yelled.

"Well we were always friends."

"I am so lost." Enzo said.

"Let me explain." God said.

"Well for starters."

"Yes?"

"Do you know the darkness that started the war?"

"Yes Quinton used to tell me and Dante stories about it."

"And?"

"I didn't think it was true."

"Well the darkness is true." God replied "The Devil is not responsible for it."

"So who is?"

Enzo got into the liking of the food and started grabbing it with God.

"Well the devil is now."

Enzo turned to see his face and saw him stuffing food in his mouth with so much sandwiches.

"The devil isn't evil."

"What are you saying?"

"I am saying that the devil was created to make people scared." God said. "It was to make sure that less people go to hell."

"Oh I see."

"Yes but when they do go to hell." God said scarily "I make sure that he punishes them for a long time."

"So that's his role."

"Yep a month in earth is a year in hell." talking with his mouth slightly full.

"By the way Enzo."

"Yes devil?"

"Now that's all your questions are answered," he said "we laughed at your girl problem."

God and the devil started having a hearty laugh over the fact that Enzo's flirting was so bad.

"Oh myself" God said "You cannot flirt at her."

"Promise me you will survive." The devil said.

"If you promise you will survive too." God replied.

The both of them seemed to be really good friends. They didn't seem to be very aggressive towards each other.

"Wait God I got a question?"

"Sure shoot away." While god drank his tea.

"What is Emily?"

God looked at the devil. "I think it is time."

"Yeah it almost is."

"What time?"

"Time for us to leave."

"It's been like twenty minutes?"

"To answer your question."

"Yes."

"She loves you."

"What?"

"She wanted to leave heaven," God said, while cleaning his mouth "just to see you again and clear the situation between you and her."

"God please tell me before you go."

"There are no tears in heaven."

"So when she saw you and Lilith together, she went to purgatory."

"Why there?"

"She wanted to cry."

"Yeah she cried on the seat when we were in our tea time."

"She still loves you."

"She still watches over you."

"Don't worry about Emily, she is one the strongest observers."

"Observers?"

"Oh myself."

"There you go."

"But he will remember, when he goes to heaven."

"He and his brother you sheltered." the devil implied. "You made him archangels."

"Oh yeah." God smiled "They were so cute."

"Yeah they were." The devil and God had a hearty smile.

"Well how do I get back?"

"Ah don't worry Enzo."

"What do you mean?"

"In death you will heal." he said. "You will die when you come here and ask for death."

"And the other way?"

"Well if you died from something you cannot recover your body."

"Damn."

"Wait I got a question!" God said.

"What for me?" a Shocked Enzo replied. "You control the earth."

"Well I am trying to strike up a conversation."

"Dev ask him a question."

"What's your cheesiest pick up line?"

God burst out laughing with the Devil.

"So funny." saying sarcastically.

Enzo liked this place and he didn't seem like he wanted to leave. He loved the food, the atmosphere and the tea.

Suddenly a question came up to Enzo's head, he wanted to know what happened to his real father. What happened to his real father how was he sent here now, when his father is somewhere on the other side. His hands trembling, sweat pouring from his palms, as he grabbed the cloth of the purest white table, licking his lips and rubbing the saliva, breathing from his mouth and exhaling through his nose as he said what he wanted "Who is my dad?"

"Which one?"

"Xander of course."

"Well." God looked across to the devil as he saw him nod his head "Tell the boy."

"Please I want to know!"

"What do you know about your father?"
"He was a leader to fight the army of darkness."
"So where is he now?"
"Oh he is busy, he is the black angel."
"The black angel?"
"The angel of death" God said.
"I cannot believe it." Enzo paused out of shock "I am death's son."

Suddenly Enzo's hand started to slowly fade away "What the?"
"Don't worry!"
"Am I going back to earth?"
"Yes you are?"
"Before you go?"
"Yes God?"
"Do you want to stay here and have tea with us for years?"
"No, I love Lilith."
"Oh my, now you have done it Enzo."
Crying noises were heard from the distance.
"What is that crying?"
"It is your former lover Enzo, Emily"
"Let me tell you something." Devil said "Every time you say I love you Lilith …"
"Don't tell me, she comes here to cry."
"Well sadly yes, I hear her almost every day when you and Lilith talk."
"She cries whenever Lilith is near you." Devil said "Emily was tasked to observe you."
"But she fell in love you."
"It is her fault!" Enzo shouted "She broke my heart and left me alone."
"Oh more girl problems."
"Well how about we go back to heaven and hell." God smiled.
"Sure."
"What about me?"
"Take a look at your body!"

Enzo looked down and didn't see his body.

"You are going home."

"Thank you God and devil."

"Sure."

"You might not remember this," the Devil said "but we will not forget you or your brother."

"By the way," God looked at Enzo in the eyes dead serious "you won the battle, not the war."

A white flash appeared in his eyes with a loud ringing noise in his ears.

Undying Love

Enzo woke up. The beeping sound of the heartbeat monitor as he slightly turned left, he saw Lilith. He slightly turned left and saw Lilith sleeping on the chair with tear marks on her cheeks. He looked around, lying down in bed and saw that the room was quite dark and alone in a small room with medical equipment. Bandages with blood on them on the floor. He lifted the sheets and saw his wounds were not recovered but it was better than before. He tried to get up but the pain brought him to the ground. Lilith woke up to the moaning as he tried to get up. She got up and eased him down getting closer and tucking him in. He looked at her in her eyes, startling her "Your eye!"

"Don't worry it comes with the package."

"What happened? Dante didn't tell me he was too upset."

"He was going to slaughter you. I couldn't let that happen."

Laying her hand on his pale face "Wow, why are you protecting me?"

"I know you are strong but I am scared of losing you."

Looking at his battered face and odd looking eyes "I love you too!"

"I know and I kept my promise."

"Never scare me like that again!"

"I love you."

Slapped his broken face "That scared me!"

She leaned forwards and said "I always wanted to do this but never had a chance."

"Me too."

Their lips collided sharing their love, passion, affection, eyes closed, touching her soft skin. She touched his rugged beard. Separating for the first time, she whispered "One more." They took their time and didn't want to leave. She left his warm lips pink and lusting for more "My love for you undying, it is enteral."

His eye glowed for a bit.

Dante opened the door and was stunned to see Enzo awake. He called Hans and Logan to check on him. Enzo pointed out "Dante your eye!"

"Yeah so is your eye."

"Is it red?"

"Yep."

"As red as blood or roses."

Having a hearty time with all of them together for the first time, after a day with Enzo in bed. Suddenly Enzo's phone rang.

"An unknown number?"

"Hello?"

"Well Enzo, you are as smart as your father no doubt and Dante is the violent part of him in which I would avoid and thank you for the delightful show."

"Who is this?"

"The leader or you thought you killed."

"What?"

"I sent a decoy or a sacrifice to test you and you are unbelievably remarkable, I won't make the same mistake twice."

He cut the call leaving him speechless as goose bumps went down his spine.

Lilith looking at the uneasiness in his face, "It's not over?"

"Don't tell me that we screwed up?"

"He tested us. It was a decoy, he knew he would lose if he fought us head on."

A moment's silence.

"What now?"

"We get stronger, smarter, better."

"But will it end?"

"It's an undying war."

"We won this one, we can win the next one."

Enzo shouted "Forget about it!"

Everyone looking towards his battered body, giving him some respect.

"Did Benjamin give us money to support us in what we did?"

"Yeah he did."

Out of sudden realization "Where is Emily?"

"She went away for some time after she found out you were almost dead."

"Alright."

Enzo ripped out all of his tubes connected to his body and ripped off the bandage.

Looking at Lilith as he stood up from his bed "Lilith!"

"Yes?"

"Let's go on our date."

"Sure."

Dante went to the grave of Quinton with flowers in his hand, removing the dead flowers. He placed them with a blue vase next to his tombstone. He removed them with the water dripping down from the steams. He threw it aside and gently placed them inside the blue vase. He knelt down and went closer to the tombstone "Don't worry old man," Dante said "I am keeping Enzo safe. Hey, I miss you and I know you were not there to see it, but Enzo moved on from Emily to Lilith and she is a fantastic woman. I really hope you were there." "I am so sorry Quinton," placing his hand on the tombstone "I didn't mean to kill you dad."

"But what I am so angry about," he looked down "Is why didn't you stop me. Just why?" But he knew that nothing could stop time or reverse time. He knew that it was done. All he knew was that he died with a smile on his face. He got up from the grave and walked over to the very stylish sports car he bought with the Benjamin funds.

Logan was with Hans and the both of them went to buy a massive house, which they wanted to be the safe house. It was the house that all their friends and new members could join in. They had everything in there that could entertain anyone and help anyone out. The both of them got friends for the first time in their pathetic lives but Hans often wondered about his dead lover. He started working on his next line of improving himself in battle. His biggest project was the blueprint in his hand as he just admires it.

Lilith and Enzo went out to the park where the sun was shining. They held hands, talking about anything that came into their minds. She went close to Enzo, as their skins were touching together. Her head resting on his shoulder. It was so much better than he could possibly remember.

Dante picked up Jonathan and took him to have ice cream and buy equipment for their new safe house with Hans and Logan. They made sure there was a secret room, in which they had their own underground garage, weapons' stash and training area.

In the distance, in the park there was a fairly young man, sitting down on the benches, looking into the distance at the landscape of where the urban city meets the river. Smirking with his hand near his chin "I underestimated them but they are clearly stupid."

A man came from behind, wearing a butler's outfit with a tray and a lid. "Sir."

He opened the lid and picked up the phone under the lid. "Yeah the war was definitely successful."

"Yes, we know how powerful they are, we are carefully planning the next course of action."

"We may have lost the battle but we will not lose the war."

He ended the call walking back.

novum PUBLISHER FOR NEW AUTHORS

Rate this book on our website!

www.novum-publishing.co.uk

The author

David Dordi was born and brought up in Dubai. He later migrated to Bristol in the United Kingdom and is currently a student. One of his favourite hobbies is playing snooker. He also likes to go forth on adventures and explore new places which is shown in his writing. "Indifferent" is Dordi's debut novel and he looks forward to writing many more.

novum 🟦 PUBLISHER FOR NEW AUTHORS

The publisher

Whoever stops getting better, will in time stop being good.

This is the motto of novum publishing, and our focus is on finding new manuscripts, publishing them and offering long-term support to the authors.
Our publishing house was founded in 1997, and since then it has become THE expert for new authors and has won numerous awards.

Our editorial team will peruse each manuscript within a few weeks free of charge and without obligation.

You will find more information about
novum publishing and our books on the internet:

www.novum-publishing.co.uk